W9-CKL-462

IRON TRAIL

IRON TRAIL

TIM CHAMPLIN

G.K. Hall & Co. • Chivers Press
Waterville, Maine USA   Bath, England

This Large Print edition is published by G.K. Hall & Co., USA
and by Chivers Press, England.

Published in 2001 in the U.S. by arrangement with
Golden West Literary Agency.

Published in 2002 in the U.K. by arrangement with
Golden West Literary Agency.

U.S. Hardcover 0-7838-9492-9 (Western Series Edition)
U.K. Hardcover 0-7540-4781-4 (Chivers Large Print)
U.K. Softcover 0-7540-4782-2 (Camden Large Print)

The text of this Large Print edition is unabridged.
Other aspects of the book may vary from the original edition.

Set in 16 pt. Plantin by Minnie B. Raven.

Printed in the United States on permanent paper.

British Library Cataloguing-in-Publication Data available

Library of Congress Cataloging-in-Publication Data

Champlin, Tim, 1937–
Iron trail / Tim Champlin.
p. cm.
ISBN 0-7838-9492-9 (lg. print : hc : alk. paper)
1. Railroads — Design and construction — Fiction. 2. Rocky Mountains — Fiction. 3. Colorado — Fiction. 4. Large type books. I. Title.
PS3553.H265 I75 2001
813′.54—dc21 2001024444

For "Aunt Margaret" Knight,
longtime friend
and granddaughter of a Western railroader.

"If you got something to say, let's hear it out loud!" said a voice from a few feet down the bar. A raised head was looking in our direction, and I knew instantly that someone had been listening to our conversation. The tension in the room was suddenly thicker than the cigar smoke as the voices at the tables quieted. I turned my head slightly without moving my hands from the bar. Two men were looking at us. I had made a casual note of their presence when we came into the hotel bar but had paid them no further mind.

"Two Santa Fe men," Gregory DeArmand said to me under his breath. The big Denver & Rio Grande stoker I had just met at supper had been filling me in on the fighting between the two rival railroads, and his bass voice had carried farther than he realized. DeArmand, who towered a good six feet four, stood between me and the two men, and I had to lean forward on the bar to see around him.

"Whatsa matter? Cat got your tongue,

Shorty?" the man taunted DeArmand. "You was sure givin' the Santa Fe hell a minute ago. Ain't got nothin' to say now?"

The man who spoke was short and stocky, with thick arms and hands, black hair, and coarse features, reddened as much by whiskey as by weather, I guessed. His companion, who was slightly taller and sported a drooping mustache, stared in our direction with a stony expression.

I glanced quickly at DeArmand. Except for a slight paling, he had not changed expression or moved. I suspected that, even though he was big and strong, he was not a rough fighter. Any confrontation would have to be with fists, since he was unarmed. I ground my teeth in frustration at not having my own Colt on my hip. I had foolishly left the heavy gun belt rolled up and stashed in my bedroll in my room upstairs. Would I never learn?

"Not so eager to shoot off your mouth now, are you?" said the stranger with the thick arms when DeArmand did not reply. "Just you keep your opinions to yourself, you big blob o' lard, or I'll shove your teeth down your throat."

DeArmand began to redden slowly at this, and I noticed his knuckles whiten as his beer mug began to tremble slightly. I was afraid the big man would explode as anger began to replace the first sudden surprise.

Apparently the two men felt they had their

man on the run because they were grinning and nudging each other.

"Give 'em hell, Bob," the mustachioed one said, turning to toss off a jigger of whiskey. The taunter was grinning and started to reply when a roar like a charging grizzly startled me. DeArmand literally leapt the few feet separating the four of us and landed on his tormentor. They crashed back against the bar. Quick as a jolt of lightning, DeArmand had his man by the arm. The next thing I saw was the stocky man sailing out across the room. He landed flat on a table, crashing to the floor as poker chips and glassware flew in every direction. The men at the table were scattering desperately to get out of the way.

A six-gun roared, and I reached instinctively for my hip as I crouched, spinning toward the blast.

But I needn't have bothered. The slim bartender with the plastered-down hair had neatly buffaloed the other man with the twin barrels of a sawed-off shotgun from behind the bar. The mustachioed one had been in the act of drawing his Colt, and the roar was the sound of his cocked revolver going off into the floor as he collapsed, unconscious.

The stocky man who had been slung into the card game was slowly extricating himself from the overturned table and chairs and the broken glass. He looked about for the gun that had somehow disappeared from his holster.

The bartender leveled the shotgun across the bar.

"There'll be no more of that in here, gentlemen," the bartender announced calmly, with a definite British accent. "If you have any differences to settle, you can bloody well take them outside into the snow."

The red-faced Santa Fe man was still looking for his gun, but the fight had obviously gone out of him. DeArmand was standing by the bar, opening and closing his huge fists, ready for battle.

"If you'll be so kind as to turn your pockets wrong side out, I'll be taking the ten dollars you owe me for damages," the bartender added to the stocky one.

"Hell, *he* attacked *me!*" the man objected, but did as he was told in the face of the dual muzzles.

I heaved a deep sigh of relief and reached for my unfinished beer. This was the second time I had assumed I was in a safe environment and had packed my gun away with my duffel. The first time had been last year in San Francisco, and it had nearly cost me my life when we were attacked by some knife-wielding Chinese assassins. I mentally vowed I would wear my gun constantly from now on, even to bed, if necessary. Helluva way to digest one's supper, I thought. I might have been better off sleeping in the stable with my horse.

DeArmand and I retired to a corner table,

where we could see the entire room, to continue our conversation undisturbed.

"Lucky we didn't get shot in that fracas," I said. "They were both armed, and we weren't."

The men in the room stopped looking in our direction and were settling back to their card games. The two Santa Fe men had gone.

DeArmand only grunted in reply. He tilted his head back and drank half of his beer at a gulp, then flicked the foam from his black walrus mustache with his other hand. He leaned forward on his elbows, and the wooden captain's chair creaked under his two-hundred-fifty-plus pounds. He was dressed in overalls and a blue woolen shirt.

"That sort of thing happen often?" I asked.

"There've been a few clashes," he replied. "But that's the first one I've been in for a long time."

"What were you telling me before those two interrupted?" I asked.

"I can't believe you signed on to work for this outfit without knowing what's been going on between these two railroads," he countered, ignoring my question and eyeing me as if I were some sort of Santa Fe spy.

"The sign said they needed laborers, and I needed a job." I shrugged. "The man in the Denver office didn't give me any details."

"Don't reckon he would, since the company's been hiring right and left. God knows why, unless it's to fight rather than work."

"Fight about what?"

"The Royal Gorge, man, the Grand Canyon of the Arkansas."

"What's this Royal Gorge? You never got around to telling me."

He looked at me incredulously. "You been living in a cave or something? Where'd you say you're from?"

I waved him off. "Just came to Denver from the West Coast a few weeks before I signed on with the Denver and Rio Grande. What is this problem between the Atchison, Topeka and Santa Fe and the Denver and Rio Grande?"

The big man seemed open and friendly when I had met him about an hour ago in the dining room. But he was a little too garrulous for me. And I was ready for bed. I'd put in two long days riding down here from Denver to Colorado City, or Colorado Springs, as it was now being called. Two days in the snow and camping by a frozen stream last night had put me in no mood for a long history discourse.

"Money," he said seriously. "Money is what it's all about. This war — that's what it amounts to, a war — between my road and the Santa Fe is over the best routes to the best-paying customers, both passenger and freight. Mostly freight. During the past few years this war has been in and out of court more times than you could shake a coal shovel at. It's kept a bunch of slick Eastern lawyers busy for years just tangling this into the damnedest mess of legal snakes you've ever seen. To put it in a nutshell, the Santa Fe is big and powerful, and the Rio Grande ain't.

"But, let me go back. . . . The trouble started when General William Jackson Palmer founded this road about eight years ago. You at least know something about that, don't you?" He arched his brows at me. Not wanting to encourage him to recite in detail eight years of the railroad's history, I nodded and grunted as if I were perfectly conversant with General Palmer's railroad.

"Well, then, you know all about how the Santa Fe beat us to the right-of-way over Raton Pass, going south into New Mexico. Well, sir, we beat *them* to surveying the only route through the Royal Gorge, west of Pueblo."

I nodded, trying to cudgel my tired mind to recall if I had read anything about all of this in the early 1870s. I vaguely remembered some controversy about it. But that seemed a lifetime ago. I had been working as a reporter in Chicago then, had never been in the West, and was not following local railroad wars with any great interest at the time. I hadn't even paid much attention to the current troubles reported in the pages of the *Rocky Mountain News* during the past two months I had spent in Denver.

"But *nobody* has ever outsmarted General Palmer. And I think he's gonna beat 'em yet. The Santa Fe forced General Palmer into bankruptcy trying to fight 'em, and the courts made General Palmer lease our road to the Santa Fe to operate, mainly because the investors were howling about the money they were going to lose. Course the head men of the Santa Fe didn't want no part of us getting back into business, so they did all they could to ruin their leased road financially — like raising freight rates to kill off business. The general raised holy hell in court about it. The judges finally saw what was happening, but they mealy-mouthed around the issue. Anyway, the whole thing has wound up on the doorstep of the Supreme Court of the United States, where it should have been long ago. And just last month they ruled on another case involving the Missouri-Kansas-Texas Railroad versus the Kansas Pacific Railway. It was mighty like our own situation, so everybody took heart that the Supreme Court will rule for us in the spring. In the meantime, those S.O.B.'s are building on the other side of Royal Gorge toward Leadville, hoping it'll strengthen their case —"

"Hold it," I interrupted him again. "Just why is this Royal Gorge so important?" I was beginning to think I might never get the straight of the story from this man. His story was jumping around. Either he was still keyed up from the brief fight or he thought I knew a lot more about this situation than I really did.

"Okay." He took a deep breath and seemed

to collect his thoughts to simplify to its basics an already simple story for the simple mind of Matt Tierney. "When we lost the right to Raton Pass, we had to look elsewhere to extend our road for revenues. The general didn't want his baby road to wind up being just a feeder line through Colorado for the major railroads. So the next best thing was to build across the Rockies, west to Salt Lake and down into New Mexico through the San Luis Valley. But our more immediate goal was to get branches into the mountain mining towns just west of here 'cause they were paying a high dollar to have their tons of ore hauled out to the smelters by mule trains and ox wagons. There's a fortune in revenues for the first road that can get a line built into places like Oroville."

"Oroville?"

"Leadville now. After gold petered out a few years back, Oroville changed its name when the miners discovered the heavy blue-black mud clogging their sluice boxes was actually rich deposits of silver and lead."

I nodded. Ouray and Silverton and Leadville were familiar names to me, although I had never been to any of them.

"Leadville, being the closest and one of the richest, was the general's first goal, but the Santa Fe fought us every step of the way. The only feasible way to build a railroad to Leadville without going a helluva long ways around is to build directly west from Pueblo, which we did several years ago. Went about thirty miles to where Canon City now sets at the mouth of the Gorge. Over the centuries, the Arkansas River has cut down through solid granite to form a groove a thousand feet deep and so narrow there's hardly room for more than the river. At most, there's room for only one set of narrow-gauge tracks — and it would take some blasting and some fancy engineering in places for that. Hell, we and the Santa Fe were tearing up each other's survey stakes and throwing each other's tools in the river seven years ago. This feud has been boiling a long time, and it's getting nastier."

"And the courts haven't settled the issue yet?" I hated to appear so ignorant of what had apparently been a major portion of this man's life, but I had been in other parts of the country at the time, doing other things.

"Not yet. The Supreme Court is due to make a ruling on it sometime this spring. Meantime, both sides are jockeying around, trying to get the best position that might influence the court's decision. That sneaky bunch from the Santa Fe has been grading and building beyond the Gorge toward Leadville, figuring if they get both feet in the door in a hurry, the court can hardly rule against them. But the weather's been holdin' them back here of late. We're all holdin' our breath about what the court'll decide, but General Palmer ain't sitting still, either. He's bound to have that right-of-way through the Gorge, come what may. And he's hiring on more men all the time to make sure of our position. I reckon that's why you were hired.

"Damn! I can hardly wait for that spring thaw!" His eyes danced with excitement as he brought his big fist down on the table, making the beer mugs jump.

I began to get an inkling of why the Denver & Rio Grande was hiring so many hands during a time of year when railroad building in this part of the country was obviously not feasible. Grateful as I was to have a job just now, it appeared that I had unknowingly hired on to fight, not to work.

I sat back and took a long swallow of my beer, taking note of the huge coal-oil chandelier that hung from the center supporting beam of the ceiling. The chandelier was set off by hundreds of cut-glass prisms that caught and reflected the light in every direction. I could hear the slap of cards behind me as the blackjack dealer worked, and the murmur of voices from the fifteen or twenty men who occupied the tables in the room. The big windows nearby were now blackened by night, but I knew they held a magnificent view of the snowy flanks of the mountains only a short distance beyond.

". . . Santa Fe bunch is brazen as hell," DeArmand was saying as my mind again focused in on his voice. "The general decided to fight fire with fire. Big companies like that think they own the whole world. Run over anybody who gets in their way — that is, if you let 'em. Sneakin' bunch has tried every illegal trick in the book to beat us out o' that Royal Gorge route. Wasn't enough they got Raton first. But they gotta have the Gorge, too. And that route is the Rio Grande's by right. We were there and surveyed that route back in '71. When it looked like they might lose out in court, the Santa Fe brought in hired guns to try to intimidate us. It didn't work. Our boys weren't gunhands, but they didn't bluff that easy. . . ."

His voice faded in my ears. I had heard it all before. My eyes were heavy with supper and the beer and the excitement and the long, cold day in the saddle. I had to get to bed.

". . . added to the fact that the general has always been hard-pressed for funds to keep building. Hell, a bunch o' the boys and I held off for three months one time on our pay when things really got tough. We wanted every cent General Palmer could scrape up from bonds or borrow to go into building more track as fast as he could finance it. I'm actually working for the Santa Fe. On paper, anyway. Ain't that a helluva note!"

By full light the next morning I had checked out and collected my bay from the Colorado Springs livery. He seemed the better for having spent a warm and well-fed night. He wasn't exactly frisky, but he seemed a lot more rested than when I had turned him over to the stable boy the night before. I grinned at the thought that this bay was no more fond of winter than I was.

The slate-gray sky threatened more snow. But the weather was always chancy this time of year along the base of the Rockies. I had toyed with the idea of laying over a day at the comfortable hotel at Colorado Springs but had decided against it. DeArmand would deadhead north this afternoon on the train for Denver, where he would fire a D&RG locomotive on the return run. And I was eager to find out what my new job in Pueblo held for me.

I took the reins, slipped a toe into the stirrup, and swung aboard. A sudden gust of wind swirled the powdery snow off the nearby roofs, and I tugged my hat down more firmly on my head. With a scarf wrapped around my ears, a heavy blanket coat, high boots, and gauntlets, I was reasonably protected from the biting air of the high plains winter.

I gave my horse his head and started south at a brisk trot, thinking, Well, Matt Tierney, what have you got yourself into now?

The gray winter morning suited my mood exactly. My close friend and constant companion of three years and several harrowing adventures, Wiley Jenkins, had married the actress, Darcy Olivia McLeod, last week and was preparing to settle into a new life and a new job as a Wells Fargo agent in Denver. I was happy for him, but feeling very sorry for myself. The chance meeting with Gregory DeArmand last night and the run-in with the Santa Fe men had only been a temporary interruption of my black mood. And now, alone again, the mood settled on me like the cold air.

I looked down at the empty leather scabbard under my leg where my rifle had rested. Being short of cash and ideas, I had given the Winchester '73 carbine, suitably inscribed, to Wiley as a wedding gift. Since he was settling down to a more civilized existence, I wondered idly if he would have as much need for it as I would. Ah, well, it would look good over his mantel.

My bedroll was wrapped in a yellow slicker behind the cantle of the worn Army saddle I rode. Packed in the saddlebags on either side were some extra clothes, a little canned food, mostly beans and tomatoes, some cornmeal, salt, a block of wooden matches, a razor, toothbrush, a small frying pan and some eating utensils, coffee and a coffeepot, and some sorghum molasses. Nearly all of my worldly possessions, with the exception of some money in a Chicago bank, were here on this horse. It gave me an empty feeling to know I had come so far and experienced so much in the last few years, had passed my midthirties in age, and had only this to show for it.

Maybe I should have stayed in Denver and looked for a job myself. The city, with its multistoried brick buildings, horse-drawn trolley, and growing population was taking on the look of the more settled cities of the East. The truth was, I really didn't want to leave my old friend. I felt I was leaving a part of myself behind. Somehow, the life that Wiley Jenkins had chosen, with all its attendant responsibility, seemed more attractive and secure than the life I was continuing to lead. Maybe I was just getting old and needed to settle down, too. Wiley was several years my junior, and he had already tired of the wild, unsettled, adventurous life. Of course, he had also started several years ahead of me. Maybe if I had fallen in love with a girl like Darcy McLeod, the settled life would have looked even more attractive to me.

I unbuttoned my heavy coat, slid my gun belt out, and looped it over the pommel. Might as well let my horse carry this two or three extra pounds. The gun was new, and I had not even fired it yet. A blued Colt .44 with a four and three-quarter-inch barrel and ivory grips, I had bought it only two weeks ago for twenty-five dollars at a Denver gun shop to replace the old army Colt I had lost last year in San Francisco when Wiley and I and two others had been attacked in the Chinese quarter of the city. That had been the beginning of the last adventure I was destined to share with my old friend, Wiley Jenkins. Even though we had left San Francisco in late October, less than four months previously, the race of the big lumber schooners on the wild Pacific and all that had gone with it already seemed long ago. But I smiled to myself at the thought that the public would not be reading my account of this intriguing adventure for another two months, when it was scheduled to appear as the lead story in the April issue of *Harper's Weekly*. They had paid me handsomely for it, with an open invitation to submit anything further I might have. Being a reporter, as I was then, had its monetary advantages.

I was the first one out on the road south since three inches of new snow had fallen last night, but I was still able to keep the trail in the treeless terrain with little trouble. I urged my bay into a lope and held that pace for about five minutes, then walked him for about twenty minutes, then repeated the procedure. I had found from experience he could travel all day at this pace, and we could eat up the ground. About once an hour I dismounted and led him, the dry snow squeaking under my boots. When the circulation and warmth gradually returned to my numbed feet, I swung up again.

Wanting to take advantage of the short daylight hours, I didn't pause for lunch but just gnawed on a piece of beef jerky and sipped ice-cold water from my canteen while riding.

Paralleling my route on the right and several miles away, bulked the ridge of the Rockies, their massive shoulders shrouded in low clouds and snow. In the afternoon the wind began to pick up, flowing down the mountain slopes and whirling the loose snow high into the air. It obscured the crystal-clear visibility like shifting fog.

The road dipped and curved in long, undulating sweeps over the alluvial plain. About midafternoon the wind brought me the far-off rhythmic chuffing of a steam engine. I pulled my bay up and dug into my saddlebag for the pair of German field glasses I carried. The twin lenses pulled the Denver & Rio Grande train into a recognizable locomotive and five cars. It was crawling north more than a mile away, black smoke whipping from its stack. It seemed to be moving very slowly, probably as a precaution against the snow on the tracks, or the engine might have been pushing a small snow plow bolted to the cowcatcher. In the rapidly failing light of the winter afternoon, the row of lighted dots that were the coach windows were a cheery sight.

The train gradually drew away and disappeared. I was sorry to see it go; it was something alive and moving against the lifeless expanse of white. By the time it was gone, I estimated I had no more than an hour of daylight left. The wind was blowing harder than ever, and snow had begun to fall again, whirling across the road and sifting into the deep wagon ruts. I felt very much alone and cold, and almost wished I had taken the clerk's suggestion to ride south in the warmth and comfort of a passenger coach. The unused pass still rested in my shirt pocket.

"I hope to hell you're worth it," I muttered just loud enough for my horse to hear.

It was an hour after dark when, through wind-lashed, watering eyes, I finally spotted two or three winking lights that marked the distant site of Pueblo.

"And to think I've come all this way just to get m'self embroiled in another fight! Damn!"

"Hell, this ain't no fight, Irishman," Tom Crenshaw, the burly foreman, replied. "We just been sent up here to do a little scoutin' is all."

The stocky, sandy-haired son of Erin snorted as the four of us piled off the handcar and tipped it off to one side of the track. "And I suppose these Winchesters are to be used for walkin' sticks, then?"

"If you work as well as you talk, you're gonna make a damn good hand," Crenshaw muttered as he hefted his rifle and trudged off toward the end of track about twenty yards away. There, a barricade of ties had been erected just past a switch that shunted any rail traffic onto a siding near Canon City.

Crenshaw, all five feet five of him, was a take-charge type of man. Short as he was, I didn't think of him as small. He was barrel-chested, with the neck of a bull and the strength to match.

The fourth member of our party, Diego Chavez, a dark-skinned, handsome man from New Mexico, was busy shoving two crowbars beneath the belt of his blanket coat, and then he shouldered a nine-pound sledgehammer.

I had spent my few days after arriving in Pueblo trying to get accustomed to my new living quarters — a four-tiered boxcar. It was one of several that had been fitted up with bunks and parked on a siding just outside Pueblo. It was clear General Palmer was putting whatever money he possessed to better use than housing his workers. The boxcar protected us from the elements outside but not from the environment inside. The car was stifling and stank of stale air, unwashed bedding and bodies, and damp wool clothing. There was a mess car where two meals a day were served, with coffee and hard bread in the morning. The car seated only about forty men at a time, so if one did not want to wait for a seat inside, he could walk outside with his tin plate and cup and eat in the cold, sitting on a stack of ties or hunkered down in the trampled snow out of the wind in whatever shelter he could find. There were no washing facilities. The men were allowed to keep a constant fire going of dead brush, logs, and old ties. This was not only for warmth, but an iron cauldron of melted snow was kept steaming over this fire night and day for anyone who wanted to dip in with pot or bucket for shaving or whatever washing he could manage or was interested in.

Of the hundred or so men, many of them recently hired, a few could afford to take rooms at a hotel in nearby Pueblo. They had to walk the mile or more to and from town every day, but mostly just to check in and let the foreman know they were on the job and available. There was really nothing much for any of us to do. Even track and roadbed maintenance was halted for the time, with the ground frozen flint-hard and the ties covered by four inches of snow.

This morning the four of us had been assigned to our first "wrecking mission" — tearing up any Santa Fe work we could find in the Gorge. In the biting wind of predawn darkness we had lashed our hand-powered vehicle to the top of a flatcar and climbed stiffly into the caboose for the twenty-five mile ride west toward the mountains. The engine and tender, three gondolas, a flatcar, and the caboose made up our little train. The friendly brakeman knew where we were bound and gestured toward the large blackened coffeepot that simmered on the potbellied stove as the train started with a jerk.

"Help yourself, gents," he offered, as he swung himself aloft into the left-side seat in the cupola. "I've got the warm job today, compared to where you're goin'."

We did as we were bid and thoroughly warmed our insides with the coffee and our backsides with the stove during the ninety-minute ride that took us across the flat, gently rising snow plain into the foothills of the Rockies. The purpose of this train was not just to give us a ride to the junction below Canon City. The train was actually being sent to collect coal to fire the D&RG locomotives. Seven years ago this part of the line had been built toward the mountains. Then, two years later, a ten-mile spur was added, branching sharply south at the small village of Florence to connect to Coal Creek Mine.

It was at the switch at Florence that we climbed out and unloaded our handcar, the four of us carrying it, our boots squeaking in the powdery snow, to set it on the westbound tracks. The brakeman heaved the stiff switch lever over and down, stamping all his weight on it to be sure it was in place before signaling the engineer to proceed. The train rolled past the switch and around the left-hand curve, and the brakeman swung aboard the caboose. Two short blasts on the steam whistle as a farewell, and the engineer gradually opened the throttle. *Whoof! Whoof! Whoof!* The train began to gather speed and pull away from us.

"Let's get to it," Crenshaw said, wrapping the wool muffler around his face as the four of us climbed aboard. It took us an hour to reach end-of-track at Canon City, an hour that saw the sun come up in a blaze of welcome from behind us, softening the ice-blue sky but warming the air not one whit.

We exchanged positions every few minutes, but by the time we reached Canon City, the icy breeze had numbed every part of exposed flesh. I had managed to keep my upper body fairly comfortable by pumping the bar to propel the handcar, but I could barely feel my toes when we finally stepped down at the end of the line.

In single file we followed Tom Crenshaw as he led the way two miles farther to the mouth of the Grand Canyon of the Arkansas. If horse, wagon, or man had come this way since the last light snowfall two days ago, the wind must have brushed out any trace of tracks. There was no way we could get lost. All we had to do was follow the Arkansas River as it plunged, roiling, out of the cleft in the mountains, rimmed with ice along its edges. For a time it seemed we were walking slightly downhill, but it was just the rock walls of the Gorge beginning to rise on either side of us that gave that illusion.

The four of us plodded on, single file, into the Gorge. Crenshaw set a fast pace, apparently trying to save daylight. I had no idea how far we had to walk. But I knew one thing — it was as far back out as it was in. We had brought blanket rolls, with some bacon, biscuit, and a frying pan, so I assumed we would be out a couple of days at least. But I was feeling good. The brisk pace helped drive the blood to my feet, which were still partially numb.

The knife-edge wind came whistling into our faces around the broken walls of naked granite.

The narrow declivity was funneling the wind down on us and there was no place for us to hide. I was bringing up the rear, but walking behind the others was no protection. I slitted my eyes nearly shut and kept my head down, but the tears were freezing on my lashes.

What a waste of time and effort this was, I thought. Even if the Santa Fe people were as deceptive and sneaky as everyone seemed to think, they surely weren't crazy enough to be abroad in such weather to be surveying, grading, or laying track. But we had been sent out on patrol to engage the enemy as if a hot war had been raging. Some of the men had come back from earlier forays and told of seeing the Santa Fe workers, who had fled on seeing our men approaching. Others, including our foreman, Tom Crenshaw, had actually exchanged a few shots from long range with the Santa Fe workers last fall. But I seriously doubted that our little expedition was anything but a wild-goose chase to keep some of us occupied and earning our five dollars per day during these last cold weeks of winter, while the management of the D&RG waited out the Supreme Court decision. At least we would have a good fighting force ready and waiting to pounce on the Gorge and hold it, no matter what the decision. Or at least that seemed to be the strongest opinion among the men during their endless hours of jawing and placing small wagers on the outcome.

There was no way we could rely on our hearing to warn us of any potential danger ahead around the sweeping curves of the gradually deepening Gorge. We all had our ears wrapped with coat collars or wool mufflers. That and the keening of the mountain wind, nearly drowned by the rushing noise of the Arkansas River beside us, smothered any but the loudest noises.

When being selected to go on this patrol, I had passed myself off as a good pistol shot, to avoid having to lug a heavy Winchester as two of the other men were doing. Even the wiry New Mexican was toting, without complaint, the few tools we had brought — short ax, two crowbars, and a sledgehammer. But, more deadly than any of us, he also carried a tightly wrapped, twelve-pound packet of blasting powder and a length of fuse.

My prowess with a six-gun had only been hinted at, but my ruse was enough to enable me to get out of any unnecessary carrying. Actually, I was no expert marksman with a handgun. In fact, I had only practiced a couple of times with my new Colt, but what difference would that make on a trip like this, where any unlikely encounter with a hostile force would be at long range anyway?

"Damnation!"

Walking with my head down and my eyes nearly shut, I had tripped over something and was on my hands and knees in the snow before I knew what happened. I had stumbled over the iron rails of a narrow-gauge track.

"Are these the rails we're to be rippin' up, now?" inquired Kerlin in his rich brogue. "This is either the end or the beginnin' of them. They don't seem to be going anywhere."

I laughed as I got to my feet, brushing off the snow. The Irishman grinned from behind the thick stubble of reddish-blond beard. His rosy cheeks above the beard attested to the cold.

"No, you thick-headed Mick!" Crenshaw shot back, not amused. "That's the track *our* outfit laid a while back."

"Oh, then we're to tear up the track that *they* laid? And just how might we be knowin' the difference? They've branded their ties, maybe? Or theirs is the four-feet eight-inch standard gauge?" He grinned again.

But Crenshaw only gave him a disgusted look and said, "Let's keep movin'. We've got a lot more ground to cover."

We walked the three-feet narrow gauge for five more miles, trudging along the outside of the rails, except in places where the roadbed ran too close to the rushing Arkansas River. Then Crenshaw crossed over to walk between the rails to avoid the treacherous footing of the ice and snow by the riverbank. At times there was barely enough room for the tracks to run between the river on the one side and the up-thrust of the sheer granite wall on the other. It was as if a giant cleaver had sliced down through the rock, so smooth and perpendicular was some of the dark granite.

I glanced up now and then, eyes slitted against the cutting wind slicing down the narrow canyon, to get an idea of where we were going. One such glimpse showed me the triangular shape of iron girders about a half mile ahead at a point where the canyon walls seemed to pinch together.

"The hanging bridge I told you about," came back Crenshaw's muffled voice as he pointed ahead. "Keep a sharp lookout. We could run into some o' those Santa Fe boys anywhere beyond that."

I had serious doubts about that, but kept my opinion to myself as we plodded on. My heart was pumping and my feet had warmed up, but the tip of my nose was freezing and running as I rubbed the back of a gloved hand across it.

"Helluva job of engineering," I remarked aloud as we approached the bridge. Chavez, just ahead of me, made no reply. At a point where there was absolutely no river-bank that could be leveled to hold the tracks, iron girders had been bolted to the rock wall, tilting sharply upward. Then, at the apex, sharply downward again, and fastened to the opposite wall. The bridge itself was suspended under this tent-shaped arrangement, one set of beams at either end and one in the middle.

As we walked out onto the middle of the bridge, which was over fifty yards long, Crenshaw paused and we came up around him.

The only sound was the squeaking of our feet in the snow and the rushing of the ice-rimmed river underneath us.

"Looks like it would have been easier to blast out a ledge to lay this track on along here," I said, blowing my nose in a bandana.

"Can't control that kind of blasting. They were afraid of damming the river if they set a charge in this granite wall," Crenshaw replied.

"We going to stop for lunch?" I asked, glancing at the sun.

"No. We got to make at least another ten miles before we bed down, and we're burnin' daylight. We'll . . . Kerlin, are you listenin'?"

"Sure, Tom. Keep talking. I'm hearing every word yer sayin'," he said over his shoulder. "You're wantin' us to walk our poor legs off and then be ready to whip all the Santa Fe boys we find at the end of it."

Crenshaw shook his head. "C'mon. Let's go."

We followed him off the far end of the bridge, the muffled thumping of our boots sounding hollow on the snowy planks.

The rest of the afternoon we wound deeper and deeper into the Gorge as the river canyon bent gradually southwest. Either Crenshaw's estimate had been wrong or it was the longest ten miles I had ever walked.

The sun had long since gone and shadows were inking in the canyon bottom, making it almost too dark to see, when we finally stumbled to a halt at Crenshaw's command.

"We'll camp here."

I could barely make out a lighter-colored jumble of rocks behind him, bisecting the level ground we walked on.

"This is the first stone fortress our men built a few years ago to hold this canyon when things got hot with the Santa Fe. This'll protect us from the wind." He dropped his blanket roll to the ground. "Tierney, you and Chavez see if you can find something to burn around here, and I'll break out the grub."

The New Mexican let the sledgehammer drop from his hand. "I have carried the heaviest load. Let the big man look for wood," he said tonelessly.

"You heard the foreman," Kerlin replied lightly. "I've carried a bigger body all day." He grinned at the dark look the smaller man gave him.

"Chavez, help Tierney with the wood," Crenshaw repeated, glancing at the two of us. Chavez dropped the crowbars, then gently unstrapped the packet of powder from inside his coat before moving away with me.

There was no wood of any size in the barren rocks, and we could find no driftwood cast up by the swiftly flowing Arkansas. We did manage to find a little dead brush in the rocky crevices along the base of the granite wall. And with this we were able to get a small cooking fire going. It was a fire that gave little light or warmth but was just enough to cook our bacon. I was ravenous and could hardly wait for the bacon to cook before snatching my portion out of the frying pan and wrapping some biscuit around it and wolfing it down. The others were doing the same, and all talking ceased while we ate, washing down our food with cold water from our canteens. We had brought along only the bare necessities, and coffee wasn't among them.

By the time we finished, our small fire was dying rapidly. I got up to scout around for some more fuel to keep it going and give some semblance of warmth. Kerlin, this time, got up to help me without a word. I got the feeling that the big, genial Irishman was just trying to get a rise out of the silent Chavez.

Searching was mostly a matter of feeling our way around, since the night had come down black in the canyon bottom. We carefully worked our way along the granite wall about a hundred yards back the way we had come.

"I think we passed some larger pieces of driftwood snagged on the rocks at a bend just before dark," I said over my shoulder to the Irishman. I was right. A few minutes later we almost stumbled over it in the dark. We kicked the jammed pile loose and began loading our arms with good-sized pieces of dry firewood.

"What brings you to this part of the world?" I asked as we worked. "Can't imagine anyone leaving a beautiful country like Ireland."

"You've been there?"

"I was born there. But my parents brought me to this country when I was just a child. I've been back about three times since to visit kinfolk, most recently about five years ago."

"Ah. Then you know the country. 'Tis a beautiful country at that, but that hardly makes up for the harshness of the life there."

"What made you leave?"

"I could see from the time I was a lad that there was little future for me there. I have six brothers and sisters, and my father only a tenant farmer and sheepherder in County Kerry. . . ."

"Oh, a Kerryman!"

"Aye. And proud I am of that fact."

"The big rocky hills and windy, grassy valleys remind me of parts of the American West."

"Ah, yes."

I thought I could detect a subtle change in his voice as he paused in his wood gathering. "The jackdaws perching on the rock chimneys in the village, the smell of the sea wind, the barking of our Border collie, Scamp, bringing the sheep down from the hills," he mused, his tone growing softer.

"The taste of a good, foamy Guinness in a pub with friends," I suggested. "The smell of turf fires on a cold, wet day."

"Aye. And the taste of m' mother's boiled cabbage and potatoes, with homemade bread." He paused again and stopped sorting out the wood. "Lord, I miss it, I do!" His voice sounded strange in the dark.

"But you asked what brought me here," he continued in a firmer tone. "I didn't come here directly from the old country. I've been gone from my home for six years. There was no future for me there, unless I had been content to work for starvation wages as a store clerk or laborer for the rest of my life. The southwest coast can be a bleak and bitter shore in the winter. There was no land for me to farm. Not that farming appealed to me anyway. Or I could have taken to the sea in a curragh as a fisherman — a hard and chancy life. I saw a chance to make some money and do a little traveling by enlisting in the British Army at the age of nineteen."

"The British?"

"They're always looking for men. And, believe it or not, there are a lot of Irishmen wearing the red."

"You've been a British soldier for six years?"

"Just took my discharge the end of last month."

"May I ask why?"

He didn't reply immediately. Both cupped arms were loaded with dead wood, and he started to walk slowly away from me back toward camp. I fell in behind him, feeling my way carefully with my feet in the dark.

"Did you ever hear of a place called Rorke's Drift?" he finally asked over his shoulder.

"No. Where's that?"

"Aye. I thought as much. It's a missionary outpost in Zululand. South Africa. Very isolated. Treeless country. Mostly a rolling, rocky plain with a few small trees along the watercourses. Some big, barren hills here and there. Anyway, on January twenty-second and twenty-third, this year, one of the biggest battles I've ever heard of or read about was fought there. And I was right in the middle of it. Maybe the news of that battle hasn't traveled this far yet, but it will. Thousands of Zulu warriors attacked one hundred and forty of us who happened to be there at the time. We were a mixed lot, with men from various regiments, most of us just stopping over on our way somewhere else. There were a few in a makeshift hospital, down with various injuries and fever. I was wearin' the chevrons of a sergeant of B Company, Twenty-fourth Regiment. We were there to repair and rebuild the Rorke's Drift mission station into a fortress, since it was in a strategic position on a deep ford of the Buffalo River."

"What got these Zulus riled up?" I directed the question at his broad back in the darkness as we shuffled carefully along the ledge by the rushing river.

"It had been building for a long time. One or two of their tribal chiefs had been whipping them up to rise up against the British, who had been dominating them for years. But we got only a short warning of the actual attack. Two messengers got through on horseback from an army encampment a few miles away and told us of a terrible massacre of our troops there — at a place called Isandhlwana. These survivors told us the Zulus were coming — thousands of them, the tall devils running and chanting all the way. The heathens had their killing blood up and were mowing down any white man in their way. We had about two hours' warning — just enough time to pull back about three hundred yards from the river where some of us were working on the approaches to the ferry and to try to form a defensive enclosure. There was a big ridge just behind the buildings that would protect us. But the other three sides were open. Our storehouse was full of meal bags and two-feet-high biscuit boxes that we used to build an enclosure connecting the main building and the storehouse and the cattle kraal. . . ."

"Kraal?"

"A cattle pen. Dutch word, I think. Like your American corral. It was a stone enclosure about five feet high.

"Mr. Witt, the missionary, and his wife were there, but Lieutenant Chard, the senior officer present, forced them to leave and head south in the only available carriage. Our total force was about three hundred and fifty men, but over half of them were a contingent of native soldiers, the Natal Kaffirs. When these Kaffirs heard that about four thousand Zulus with the blood lust on 'em were bearing down on us, they simply vaulted over the wall and deserted en masse. Of the one hundred and forty men we had left, thirty of them were disabled in various degrees and were in the hospital. When I realized what was facing the few of us, I got cold chills all over. I tell ya, Matt, I heard the angels whisperin' m' name that day. Why I didn't leave my bones on the African plain I'll never know. But I'm still here, and I hope to stay around awhile longer. I thought I'd just about used up my share o' luck after that fight, so I took my discharge soon after and caught a Capetown steamer for New Orleans."

"It was really that bad?"

"Bad?" He stopped and turned around so suddenly that I bumped into him. "Bad? I don't want to be accused of exaggeratin', but I don't think I have the words to describe what happened that day and night. It was as close as I'll ever come to hell on earth. I still see those awful sights in m' nightmares. You might say it scared me right back to church, it did."

Just then we reached the dark camp and dumped our load of driftwood next to the stone barricade.

"Good. You got some wood," Crenshaw said. "That oughta keep us warm part o' the night." He proceeded to feed the few glowing embers that were winking red in the fitful night wind, and in a few minutes the fire was blazing up, bright and cheerful. I could then see clearly the rock wall of the hand-built fortress where we sat was composed of broken rocks stacked about four feet high and two feet thick, extending out from the base of the canyon wall almost to the riverbank. The heat of our fire was reflecting off this wall and thoroughly warming us. Crenshaw dug out a short pipe, packed it with Lone Jack, and lighted it. He leaned back against the rock wall, puffing contentedly, his big coat thrown open to admit the warmth.

Chavez sat on the other side of him, his handsome face etched in bright light and shadow, black eyes staring into the flames, seeing some vision in his mind's eye.

"Finish your story," I urged Kerlin as the big Irishman finished stacking some small logs close at hand. He shrugged out of his coat, revealing a dark blue double-breasted shirt and galluses. He sat down next to the wall and proceeded.

"I tell ya, Matt, it was eerie. It gives me the chills even now, just t' be thinkin' of it. There we were, the bunch of us, spread out behind that wall of biscuit boxes and meal bags and the two buildings in that compound, awaitin'. It wasn't cold, but we were sweatin', I can tell you. It must have been an hour or so, but it seemed like an eternity, before we heard 'em coming. It sounded like a train in the distance — a steady, rhythmic chanting of thousands of voices. It got gradually louder and louder, and finally they appeared over the crest of a knoll several hundred yards away, like all the devils of creation had suddenly risen straight up from the bowels of hell. I could almost feel my hair raising my sun helmet up off my head. But they didn't attack at once. No, they stopped for a few minutes to prepare with some kind of ritual chant. A leader's voice would sing out something, and then the rest o' them would answer. This went on for a good ten minutes. It sounded almost like a Latin litany in church — a mighty barbaric litany. They may have been resting from their run.

"While all this was happening, I had a chance to study them through the field glasses. Damn near every one o' those heathens was tall — six feet and up as near as I could tell. All the Zulu warriors I had seen up to that time were tall men. They were all painted up for battle and had all kinds of bracelets and ostrich feathers hanging from their arms and legs. Nearly every one of them carried an assegai, a throwing spear, and a hide-covered wooden shield painted up with symbolic figures. It didn't make me feel any easier once I had seen 'em close up through the glasses, you can bet.

"Every man of us was lookin' to his arms. We had single-shot Westley-Richards rifles that were accurate at long range, but they tended to jam if shot continuously. And for a side arm we had Adams Mark II revolvers. We were pretty well supplied with ammunition. Well, just about then, one of our sentries came running up from the river, yelling, 'Here they come — black as hell and thick as grass!'

"They came loping down that long, grassy hill from two directions. Then I knew what had sounded like a train earlier — they were rapping their spears on their shields in unison. Without actually hearing it, you can't imagine what that sounds like when thousands of them are doing it in rhythm and yelling at the same time."

"Sounds a little like the Battle of the Rosebud," I muttered, shuddering inwardly at the thought of the Sioux and Northern Cheyenne attack I had endured nearly three years before in southern Montana Territory.

"They attacked in waves," Kerlin continued. "And we mowed 'em down like wheat. We had firearms and they had spears, mostly, but the odds were about even since they outnumbered us at least thirty to one. After a few minutes the powder smoke was so thick you could hardly see more than a few yards in any direction. There was still plenty of daylight in the late afternoon, but there was no wind to blow the smoke away.

"After the first attack they pulled back and re-formed and hit us again. This time our outer defense buckled, and our men had to retreat back to a smaller enclosure of meal bags. These biscuit boxes and meal bags weighed about a hundred pounds apiece, so they made a good barricade. Smoke was everywhere, chokin' us, stingin' our eyes. After about two hours of repeated attacks, my throat was so dry I would have sold my soul for a drink of water. Cool as it was, sweat was pourin' down my face. But they kept acomin', wave after wave of 'em. And we kept shootin' them until our rifle barrels were so hot we couldn't touch 'em. Those buggers were walkin' on the bodies of their fallen mates. It was awful!" He shook his head at the memory and stared at the leaping flames before him.

"But the worst attack came after dark. We had lost several men and couldn't man the entire perimeter, so some of us had pulled back into the mission building, where the men in the hospital who were able were given guns to defend themselves. The building was a jumble of rooms, some of them connected, some not."

"Most American Indians wouldn't have attacked at night," I commented.

He nodded. "But they came at us again off that knoll, keeping up that infernal chanting, rapping those spears on their shields until they got right up to the compound. Then those black devils slid right up to the loopholes and windows before we knew they were there. Many of our men were wounded and about fifteen killed — run through by those damned spears or shot with rifles the Zulus had stolen from the other detachment they had overrun. They threw torches on the thatched roof, and the blaze lighted up the place like daylight.

"We barricaded the doors with chairs and tables and mattresses. But their sheer weight of numbers finally burst in the doors. We cut 'em down as they forced their way in, one and two at a time. We chopped our way with a pick through the walls and dragged the wounded from room to room, fighting a rear guard action with pistols and rifle butts and bayonets. Blazin' pieces of the ceiling were falling in on us. We finally escaped out the window of the last room and joined our mates inside the small perimeter. We were just tryin' to stay alive from minute to minute. I didn't expect to see another sunrise, I can tell you. But somehow we beat 'em off before they got all of us. They pulled back about one and a half hours before daylight. We were exhausted. While we waited for the next attack, some of our men fell asleep over their rifles. But the next attack never came.

"The sun finally came up, all bloody red through the smoke. The fifty or sixty of us still on our feet were numb with shock and fatigue, our faces and hands all covered with the greasy black residue of burnt powder. Some were bleedin' from various cuts and wounds. We wandered outside to take stock. Lord, 'twas a sight to behold! Hundreds of dead Zulus everywhere, inside and outside the enclosure, like black peat slabs fresh cut from the bog and piled in the sun to dry. I couldn't believe the rest of the Zulu warriors had actually gone. But gone they were, and all of us gave thanks for that fact.

"I couldn't believe we had survived. When the realization finally hit me, I made up my mind right then I'd had enough and was going to get out. I didn't think my luck would last another siege like that. As soon as we were sure they were gone, we buried our dead and made our way back south toward Capetown. Met up with reinforcements on the way. But my hitch was up, and I took a discharge. I heard about a dozen of our men, both living and dead, were nominated for the Victoria Cross for unusual bravery in the face of the enemy. There *were* a lot of brave, selfless acts, one man helping another, y' know, and all helping the wounded. But it was mostly sheer desperation, rather than bravery, I'm thinkin'.

"The British gained nothing from the war, and the Zulu nation gained nothing but the loss of some o' their best men. There's going to be more fightin'. I'm just glad to be away from it. The whole business was so senseless.

"And now here I am, in another fightin' situation. And I thought railroad buildin' would be a welcome change. After all, the first railroad might not have been built across this country if it hadn't been for a few thousand of my displaced countrymen."

He shook his head and poked up the fire, throwing on two more pieces of wood from the pile beside him. The dry driftwood caught and blazed up, throwing us all into brighter light. No one spoke for a few minutes. I'm sure it was the first time Tom Crenshaw had heard this story of Kerlin's recent past. Until now, Mike Kerlin had just been a big, joking, sandy-haired Irish laborer. Somehow, this harrowing tale had put him in a totally different light.

"Reminds me of tales I've heard of the Alamo," I mused.

"I remember reading a brief article about that a few weeks back when I was in Denver," Crenshaw finally remarked. "But there wasn't much detail. You were damn lucky."

The Irishman nodded. "I still don't know what made them pull back like that. They would have had us all for sure if they'd a kept comin'. Maybe some superstition. But, as I think back on it, it was more likely some of their leaders called it off. Probably thought we weren't worth the losses they were taking.

"Besides my memories, here's the only souvenir I kept of that fight." He opened a flapped holster at his belt and pulled a revolver. A lanyard ring was fastened to the butt of the weapon. "Should've turned this in, but in all the confusion, I just shoved it in my duffel. B'God, I figured the queen's forces at least owed me this. Standard-issue side arm — a John Adams, six-shot, .450 caliber." He slid the pistol back into its leather sheath.

After a few more minutes of silence, Crenshaw knocked the dottle out of his pipe on the rock wall behind him, stretched, and yawned. “I don’t know about you boys, but I’ve had a long day. Think I’ll get me some shut-eye.”

We followed his lead and rolled into our blankets out of the wind as near the fire as we dared. I was asleep before I realized how tired I was.

The cold drove us out of our blankets some time before daylight. We stirred up the fire and fried some more bacon before a wintry morning light began filtering into the depths of the canyon.

"A good, hot pot o' tea would surely go down well this mornin', lads," Kerlin grinned as he stretched the stiffness from his limbs. "I'm not complainin', mind ya," he hastened to add as Crenshaw frowned in his direction. "Like I said last night, I'm just glad to be here. Mother of God, I'm glad to be anywhere — alive — after Rorke's Drift!" He grinned.

Breakfast was the same as supper — bacon and dry biscuit, washed down with cold canteen water. We scooped some river water on our fire and were on the trail again by the time the light was good enough to see well.

Diego Chavez had spoken very little since we left Pueblo. Either he was a very quiet person by nature or perhaps wasn't comfortable with English. More than likely, he wasn't comfortable in the company of three gringos. His silence didn't really matter, since Kerlin talked enough for both of them.

I estimated we had covered about two miles along the edge of the river when we came upon some survey stakes that Crenshaw said had been placed by the Santa Fe.

"Take it mighty easy from here on," the foreman cautioned. "Keep a sharp lookout."

We proceeded a little more carefully, but the Gorge still seemed empty and lifeless, held in the icy grip of old man winter. The sun had risen so that it shone its pale light down into the canyon, but again it brought no warmth.

A short distance on, we suddenly came to the spot where a track-laying crew had stopped work. The ground showed signs of having been leveled, and then rough-hewn ties had been placed down and partially ballasted for about forty yards before we reached the end of the spiked narrow-gauge rails. We kept walking silently, sometimes stepping between the rails when the ledge was too narrow for safe footing.

We had covered slightly more than a quarter-mile when Crenshaw held up his hand and we halted.

"Hear that?"

I strained my ears but could distinguish nothing over the rushing noise of the Arkansas River beside us. There was a bend in the canyon ahead of us, and we went slowly forward, rifles at the ready, watching the heights above us as well as the canyon in front.

Even before we rounded the next curve about fifty yards on, I began to hear what Crenshaw had heard — noises of mules braying, human shouts, and what sounded like the cracking of whips. The sounds came as a jumble of faint echoes. We crept around the next bend, and all we beheld was a vista of more canyon. But it was different from the sheer gorge we had been traversing. The sheer granite walls had drawn apart, and up ahead they angled back from the perpendicular. The walls were just as high as before but they were cracked and seamed and weathered by many such winters as we were now experiencing, and many torrential rains and many blistering suns. Rock had decomposed, and windblown dust had settled in the thousands of cracks. Bushes and small trees had taken root and grown to further widen the cracks until slabs of rock had split off and fallen. Sandy soil and brush and big chunks of rock now formed a mounded footing on each side of the river, curving up a hundred feet or so before abutting against the sheer rock face. It looked as if the earth and brush and rocks had been piled on either side to help hold up the massive nine-hundred-foot cliffs. Some fair-sized trees screened the canyon ahead, but I could hear the sounds clearer now — the unmistakable sounds of men and animals working.

Crenshaw gave us a hand signal and we left

the level track and began climbing the rough talus slope. The rushing of the river and the wind blowing into our faces masked any small noises we made. We stayed low and crept along among the massive broken rocks and never went above the level of the treetops about fifty feet above the river. As the noise got closer, we crept from rock to rock. I wasn't sure if any guards or lookouts had been posted, but we saw no one. But that didn't mean they weren't there, somewhere.

Finally we spotted mule teams in the distance, pulling scrapers. Human figures, looking small in the distance, swarmed along a flat stretch by the river and around a bend out of our view upcanyon. I was glad I had thought to bring my field glasses and dug them out of the small pack I carried and focused on the activity below. I immediately felt uneasy when the figures jumped into sharp focus, seemingly much closer. It was as if they could see me as clearly as I could see them. Teams of men and animals were dragging boulders out of the way, cutting and burning brush, grading and smoothing the rough right-of-way. Closer to us, where the right-of-way had been prepared, ties were being set. I made a quick mental estimate of the men I could see between the wind-tossed treetops and the bend of the canyon. Then I handed the glasses across to Crenshaw, who lay next to me beside a slab of rock. I guessed there were at least three hundred men within my view, and maybe fifty teams of horses and mules. It was clear I had been wrong in my estimate of the Santa Fe. They were definitely out and working in this winter weather, determined to get a jump on the D&RG as well as the decision of the high court.

Crenshaw studied the scene, carefully shielding the lenses with his hands to prevent any reflection of the sun off the glass.

Finally, he motioned with his head and the four of us bellied backward among the rocks and brush until we could creep down the slope the way we had come.

"Just what I suspected," Crenshaw said when we were back a safe distance near the end of the track. "They're out in force, trying to get as much track laid as possible. Well, we'll just have to undo some of their hard work. Chavez, dig out those crowbars and sledge and we'll put a few of these rails in the river."

Diego got the tools from a crevice in the rocks where we had left them before our climb. Chavez silently handed me and Kerlin each a crowbar and took the nine-pound sledge himself. Crenshaw gripped his Winchester and walked a few yards away, watching, his gaze sweeping the high canyon rims above and the bare trees along the river.

Kerlin and I fell to on either side of a rail, levering the frozen spikes loose from the ties, a difficult and agonizingly slow job. Chavez helped by swinging his sledge against the rail, once we had loosened the few spikes that held it. For the next thirty minutes there was no sound but the spanging ring of the sledge against the rails and our heavy breathing as we grunted and sweated under our heavy coats to pry up the spikes from the frozen wood.

Crack! Boom! Boom! Boom!

We were scrambling for cover before the echoes of the shot died.

Scuttling on hands and feet, I managed to get behind a huge slab of rock that rested on the talus slope to my left.

Whang! Boom! Boom! Boom!

A second rifle slug clanged off an iron rail.

Diego Chavez dropped his sledgehammer with a grunt of surprise and pain. He was standing outside the track when the shots came and had just straightened up when the second ricocheting bullet hit him. He slipped on the icy bank of the river and in an instant was gone from sight.

"Cover me!" I yelled.

The roar of rifle fire started from either edge of the boulder where I lay as Crenshaw and Kerlin opened up on the unseen gunman above and upcanyon of us. I made a dash for the riverbank, diving and rolling over the edge, clawing at the dead brush on the bank with my gloved hands to keep from going down into the river. Another bullet kicked icy pellets into my face as I slid down the steep bank that afforded some partial cover. I stopped just short of the rushing water. The New Mexican had broken a thin crust of ice and lay half in, half out of the water, weakly trying to pull himself back up. I grabbed him by the collar with my right hand and dug my heels into the soft snow and frozen gravel under it. He didn't move. He was not a big man, but his heavy clothing was partially water-soaked, and he was apparently stunned by the lead slug and the numbing cold and was unable to help me much. I had to get him up that bank and under cover, somehow, before the marksman found us. And I didn't really know where the gunman was. I guessed he was somewhere above us.

"C'mon, Diego, push!"

I didn't know how badly he was hurt, but as I reached back to get a grip on his coat with both hands, he winced slightly in pain, even as he tried to struggle up the slippery bank. I saw no sign of blood, and his black eyes registered no feeling at all.

The firing had stopped for a few seconds, and I could hear the wind whistling through the dry brush just above my head. I heaved with all my strength, bracing my legs, and managed to drag Chavez up out of the water onto the frozen gravel. His teeth were beginning to chatter. I inched up until my eyes were just above the edge of the bank, my hat screened somewhat by the dead brush between the embankment and the track we had been tearing up.

I could see Kerlin and Crenshaw crouching behind the huge granite slab, glancing in my direction and then in the direction of the sniper. As I turned to slide back down, the gunman's rifle exploded again, the slug whining off a rock near my head. The answering echoes slammed back and forth from the canyon walls, dying away to an eerie silence once more.

Sweat was drying cold on my body. What a helluva spot! Pinned down with a wounded man who was very likely beginning to freeze to death as well. In a remote canyon with an unseen rifleman trying to kill us — a rifleman who had all the advantage of concealment and a good vantage point, I had no idea what my next move would be.

I couldn't stay where I was. I had to get Chavez to cover and tend to his wound. But how? I eased back up until my head was just below the lip of the bank.

"Can you see him?" I yelled across at my two companions.

"No. Just a puff of smoke up there in the rocks above the trees."

"Can you keep him pinned down while I drag Chavez over there?" I yelled back.

"I think so," Crenshaw said.

The winter sun was high in the sky by this time and was shining down into the canyon, giving a false impression of warmth. The blues and grays of the ice and shadows had mostly been erased. The hidden gunman would have no difficulty seeing us. He had come very close, shooting downhill from a distance of at least four hundred yards, I estimated, measuring the shot with my eyes as I studied the spot that Crenshaw had pointed to. It was a place of rugged, broken rocks and boulders, where the sheer wall had broken down and scaled off, forming the beginnings of a slope that curved down into the trees bordering the river ahead of us.

I slid on down to the gravel bar where Chavez lay. He had pushed himself to a partial sitting position and was leaning over, seeming to favor his left side.

"Can you stand up?"

He nodded. His black eyes still showed no pain or fear. He had not spoken a word or made a sound since the careening bullet had struck him.

"Is it bad?"

"I don't think so." His voice sounded steady but rather weak.

"C'mon, we have to get you to shelter."

I crouched beside him, my boots in the edge of the water. I reached around his waist, pulling his right arm around my neck. He let out a gasp as both of us lifted him to a standing position. I expected any second to feel a bullet slam into me from the sniper. But no shots came. Apparently, the steep bank sheltered us somewhat from his angle of fire.

"Now, easy does it." I half dragged him several feet up the incline where we sagged against the lip of the bank. I was panting.

"Okay, now. You'll have to help me. We have to get from here across that open space over the tracks into the shelter of that big rock. Think you can make it?"

He nodded. His eyes seemed alert. There was

no sign of shock or hypothermia as yet. By God, this little man was tough!

"Kerlin! Crenshaw! Have you got plenty of ammunition to cover us when we make a break for you?"

"You got it. Just say the word."

I heard two levers work almost as one as the rifles were cocked. I reached around Diego's waist again with my left arm and got a grip on his belt under the big, wet coat. I draped his right arm around my neck again and took a deep breath, bracing my feet on the slope. Here we go, I thought. "I hope to hell we catch him napping up there," I muttered. "NOW!"

I yanked the smaller man up for the sprint. But it was more of a stagger. We stumbled and fell into the dead brush.

The roar of rifles drowned everything as our men laid down a withering fire against the area where they had last seen smoke. I jerked Chavez to his feet and lunged forward again. It was like trying to run in a dream. I willed my legs to move but couldn't run. The New Mexican was doing his best to help, but most of his weight was on me. I didn't hear the shots but saw spouts of snow and gravel erupting in front of me. There was no way I could zigzag to throw off the sniper's aim. It was get to shelter of the boulder fast or not at all. As we crossed the tracks, Chavez tripped, and I had to stop suddenly to keep him from falling. Just at that second a slug plowed into one of the ties between the rails just where I would have been had we not jerked to a stop. This rifleman was good!

"Run, Diego, run!"

His legs began to move in a limber gait, in response to my shout in his ear. The slab of rock came gradually closer. The blasting of the covering fire was louder as the shots blended with the echoes into one continuous roar. A bullet tugged at my pants leg and clipped the edge of my boot sole. We made one last desperate rush for the shelter of the cabin-sized boulder.

We rolled to safety just as a slug chipped the edge of rock and whined off into the distance. I lay on my back, panting. Crenshaw and Kerlin stopped firing, and booming echoes ricocheted back and forth until they were swallowed by the silence of the canyon.

"Think you might have got him?" I finally managed to gasp as I sat up.

"Naw. If we did, it was only a lucky shot. He was still gettin' off shots at you," Crenshaw said. "He was probably movin' around up there behind those rocks. We were just trying to scatter enough lead around to make him keep his head down."

He turned to us. "You two okay?"

"Yeh," I nodded. "Better check Chavez, though. He took a slug somewhere. And we better get him outa those wet clothes before he freezes."

The blond-bearded Irishman was still crouched at the edge of the rock, thumbing

.44-40 cartridges into the loading gate of his Winchester with cold-reddened fingers. After the crashing roar of gunfire, the sudden stillness seemed almost eerie.

"We'll have to cut these damn boots off," Crenshaw growled, reaching for his knife. "They're already hard as a rock."

As I crawled over to Chavez, he was shaking uncontrollably, his lips a bluish color.

"Can you feel your toes?"

He shook his head.

"We need to get a fire going," I said to Crenshaw. "You got any matches?"

He nodded. "There's a block in my coat pocket."

I was able to crawl on hands and knees and gather some dead, dry brush and still remain under cover. But the brush would flare up and burn out quickly. We needed something more substantial to burn. Some roughhewn ties lay scattered about where track-laying work had stopped, near the spot where we had begun ripping up the rails.

"See anything of that maniac?" I asked Kerlin as Crenshaw began hacking at the frozen boots.

"Nothing."

"I've got to make a grab for a couple of those ties. Keep me covered."

"Ready?"

He nodded.

"Now!"

The rifle cracked again and again as fast as he could work the lever and I made a dash for the loose ties.

The cover was effective, since no answering fire came. Or else the gunman had retired. I was able to drag two of the ties to shelter without drawing any red-hot slugs. By then Crenshaw was attempting to get the New Mexican's clothing off, thin ice cracking from his pants as he pulled them down. Only the tail of the blanket coat seemed to have gotten wet. As we rolled him out of the coat, something fell on the ground.

"Damn! I forgot about that pack of black powder. Is it still dry?"

I felt it. "Seems so." Chavez had carried it tied around his body just above his waist, and it had not been submerged. Its tight oilskin wrapping was a little damp on the outside, but I doubted that any moisture had penetrated.

Even with his razor-sharp hunting knife, Crenshaw had trouble slicing through the iron-hard leather of the frozen boots. But the two of us finally managed to get the boots off without hurting the man's legs or feet. His dark skin looked pale and bloodless when we finally removed the wool socks. We stretched his shaking, naked body on the wool lining of Crenshaw's big sheepskin coat, which he had spread on the ground, and wrapped him in it, then rubbed his feet and legs vigorously.

"Stay on guard, Kerlin," the foreman ordered, "while we thaw him out."

I secured the block of matches from Crenshaw's coat pocket and crumbled some of the dry brush in my hands, along with some dead grass that was poking through the snow near the base of our great slab of rock. Using this as tinder, I broke a match off the block, cupped it out of the draft, and struck it on a small rock. The dry grass flared and I carefully fed it twigs, coaxing the blaze into heartier life. I borrowed Crenshaw's knife and sliced some slivers of dry wood from the splintery ties and added those.

Warming Chavez up could now be accomplished but his wound was another matter. There was considerable blood down the left side of his chest, but until Crenshaw began carefully wiping it off, I couldn't tell where it was coming from. As I slowly built up the fire, I watched the foreman cleansing Chavez with a touch as gentle as a woman's. I breathed a sigh of relief when I saw that the wound was above the collarbone. It had very nearly missed him altogether. The heavy slug had ricocheted off the iron rail, losing some of its momentum and then had penetrated a heavy coat and the muscle at the very top of his shoulder. Crenshaw had stopped the remainder of the bleeding with handfuls of snow. When we eased Chavez over, we could see no exit wound. The bullet, or a fragment of it, since it didn't appear to be large enough for a .44, was still lodged in the muscle.

"What about it, Kerlin?" Crenshaw called, not taking his eyes from his patient.

"Quiet as a church," the Irishman reported. "He's either stopped one of our lead messengers or he's decided to challenge something with a little less venom."

"Or he's circling around trying to get a better shot at us," the foreman growled. "Keep your eyes peeled."

I had wrapped Chavez's legs and feet in my own coat, and the fire was now blazing up cheerfully, forcing the heavy cold back a few feet. We brought the wounded man as close to it as we dared. We propped him up as best we could, shielding his naked body from the swirling wind that still blew down the canyon. With the fire, and a rubbing of his limbs, we soon had blood coursing through his veins and bringing the life-giving warmth back to the surface. His lips lost their bluish cast, and the glassy look vanished from his eyes as he started to take an interest in his surroundings. I gave him sips of water from my canteen, and soon had him gnawing on a dry biscuit and a piece of jerky. He sat on my coat, facing the fire, with his knees drawn up, and Crenshaw's coat thrown around his shoulders. Even though he had to be feeling some pain from the lead in his shoulder, he never let on. His only concession to pain was holding his left arm crooked close to his body. He had the stoicism of some Indians I had encountered.

My cotton long johns and my double-breasted woolen shirt were not shutting out the cold, and I had to keep turning first one side and then the other to the flames.

"Who do you think that was up in those rocks?" I asked.

"Santa Fe men," Crenshaw replied immediately, as if there were no doubt.

"Men? You think there was more than one?"

The foreman shrugged. "Could have been. Somebody was getting off shots at you, even though the two of us were spraying that spot with lead. And I could have sworn I saw two puffs of smoke at the same time."

"You reckon they were just trying to scare us off?"

"Not a chance. If they'd wanted to scare us off, they'd've hollered a warning first, same as they did last year before things really got heated up."

"Shootin' to kill over some damned, worthless iron rails? Rails they may not even own the right-of-way for?" This kind of killing over property rights had always baffled me. I could understand hanging a man for horse stealing, since a man's transportation in this country often meant his life. Or shooting another man in self-defense. But this? Until we had encountered the large work force, I fully expected to see no one and hear no one this day. Crenshaw seemed not at all surprised at the attack, as if he had expected it all along. But then, he had

had dealings with the Santa Fe men before, and I had not.

"The Santa Fe has hired some of the meanest gunhands in the Territory," Crenshaw continued, as if reading my thoughts. "Instead of having workmen doubling as gunhands, like they used to, they now have gunmen making a pretense at being workmen."

Kerlin finally leaned his Winchester against the rock and came over to extend his reddened hands toward the fire.

"What now, lads? Not a sign of that devil up there."

"Could be he's waitin' us out, but I'd say more likely they've gone," I opined.

"If so, I'm sure they've left a guard to make sure we don't tear up any more track or pull up any survey stakes," Crenshaw said. "They were put there to make sure none of the Rio Grande men came any farther up this gorge, and they did their job well, blast their hides! Lucky one of us wasn't killed."

I glanced at the overhead light. The pale winter sun was well past meridian. Deep in the canyon, the afternoon shadows of the short day were stretching out.

"We need to make it back downriver as far as we can before dark," I said.

"Chavez has no clothes, and that wound of his . . ."

I thought of the several miles of twisting canyon we had traversed coming in. With our handcar, and rails all the way, getting out would have been a cinch. But that was only wishful thinking.

There was silence for a few minutes as we pondered the dilemma. Even if Chavez could summon up the strength, walking on the rocks and snow barefoot was out of the question. If we stayed where we were overnight, we would still be in danger of the unseen riflemen. And it was possible that the New Mexican's wound would stiffen up or start to become infected, so that we might have to wind up carrying him all the way back.

"Let's use one of the blankets," Kerlin finally said.

We looked at him curiously.

"Cut it up. Wrap his feet and legs," he explained. "Except for the blood, his shirt's still dry. We can rig up something."

"And he can wear my coat," I added. "I can move fast enough to stay warm. What about it, Diego?"

"*Sí.* I am ready. *Vamanos.*"

It was a matter of only a few minutes' work for me and Kerlin, with Diego's help to cut a blanket into strips, winding them around feet and legs and tying them with smaller strips. Crenshaw took a rifle and stood guard near the rock while this was being accomplished. We bound dry pieces of Diego's undershirt around the wounded shoulder and across his body before he slipped back into the shirt that was partially stiffening with dry blood. We gave Kerlin his big sheepskin coat back, and the New Mexican took mine, since it wasn't quite as heavy. We tried to force him to eat as much as he could hold of the jerky and biscuit, but after a few bites he held up his hand. "No more, amigos. My stomach . . . it feels . . . *muy mal.*" He had begun to look a little pale. I again had reason to regret that we didn't have some good, strong coffee to give him.

"Ready to travel? Let's move out." Crenshaw led the way as we started back down the long trail we had come. We took the rifles but left the crowbars and sledgehammer as unnecessary encumbrances. We also added two more ties to our fire and left it burning, just in case someone might be watching the smoke from a distance. And, in case they didn't see us slip away, they might be fooled by the light of the fire after dark. It was a slim hope.

Our pace was slower, even though we were now going gradually downhill and had the sharp wind at our back. We walked single file again, with Crenshaw leading and Kerlin bringing up the rear. I lugged the twelve-pound bundle of black powder just in case we had to use it for something before we got out.

There was no warning. I was walking only three feet behind Chavez when his knees buckled and, with something like a sigh, he crumpled facedown on the trail, his head just missing a sharp rock as his hat rolled away.

I was at his side in a second and rolled him over. My hand touched the sticky wetness under the coat where his wound had broken open and was oozing again. "Passed out," I said. "Maybe just weakness from loss of blood. I think he's about done in for the day."

"We'll camp here," Crenshaw said. "It's almost dark, anyway. Let's scout up some firewood."

While Kerlin and I tended to this chore, I slid the unconscious man around a projecting shoulder of rock as a partial protection from the wind, and started to check the man's wound. I slipped my coat off his shoulders and shrugged into it myself since the wind was chilling the perspiration on my body. I carefully peeled off the torn undershirt bandage and then took some handfuls of snow and pressed them to the wound to stop the slow bleeding again.

As I was turning him over, I felt something rough on his back. The dying light revealed a mass of scars from the shoulders to the waist. The scars were not noticeable from a distance but up close they didn't seem to be scars from some sort of pox or disease. The rest of his skin was perfectly smooth and clear. In all other respects, Diego Chavez was a very handsome, well-formed man. I looked closer at his back. Besides the crisscrossing of hundreds of small marks and scars that appeared to have been made with a lash, the raised scar tissue my hand had first encountered was somewhat larger and formed in a regular pattern. Turning him toward the last of the fading twilight, I could just trace the pattern with my eyes. It was three long, parallel scars perpendicular, crossed with three more long, parallel scars horizontal. Something very painful had happened to this man. What it was I couldn't imagine. Had he suffered this in some prison? Or was it some corporal punishment dealt him at sea?

But just then he groaned and his eyes fluttered open. I draped his shirt over his back again.

"Ah, Matt, I am sorry, amigo. It was weak of me to . . ." He paused and took a deep, shuddering breath and expelled it.

"Don't try to talk. Just lie still, and we'll have a fire going shortly."

"Such a small thing is this tiny bullet. And I am acting like a small child. I have suffered much worse pain than this. . . ."

I could well believe it after seeing his back, but I said nothing. For some reason I couldn't explain to myself, I didn't want him to know I had seen the scars. Maybe I would ask him about that later. But, as the others returned with some dry wood, I knew this wasn't the time or the place.

Even with the life-giving warmth of a blazing fire, this was going to be a very uncomfortable night, exposed as we were to the wind.

We cooked up the last of our bacon and passed around the crumbling remains of the biscuits. I tried to coax Diego into eating small portions of the food slowly, which he did. His stomach seemed settled once he had stopped walking, and before our meager meal had been long over, his head was lolling back on the blankets. I made him as comfortable as I could, covering him with my own blanket to try to keep as much warmth in his body as possible. He fell asleep quickly.

After several minutes I signaled for the other two to move away on the other side of the fire. Crenshaw looked curiously at me as he held a blazing twig to his ever-present pipe and puffed it into life.

"What's the situation?" I asked Crenshaw. "This man won't stand too much more of this. We're out of food, and we've still got a long way to go to reach our handcar at Canon City."

Crenshaw removed the short pipe from his mouth and spat to one side. "I'm well aware of our situation. But there's nothing for us to do but keep going. That bullet isn't in a vital spot, but I don't care to risk trying to dig it out. Do you?"

I shook my head.

"We're at least a good twelve miles from Canon City, and you both know the terrain. But we're going downhill, so the walking will be somewhat easier — a drop of about two thousand feet. We may have to take turns carrying him. Or we might have to rig a travois if we can find some poles. It'll be tough, but we'll make it. We've got plenty of water. I think Chavez will stand the trip. I wish to hell I'd been more alert. I might have prevented this. I might have known they'd have sentries posted."

"Lads, I hate to bring this up, but while I was watching our back trail today, I could swear I saw someone following us. He dodged out of sight as soon as I looked around. We're not alone in this canyon. Whoever it was, certainly didn't want to be seen, I can tell you."

"You sure you weren't mistaken?"

"No, indeed. I caught sight of him about three times."

We looked silently at each other. If we were to survive this night, it appeared we would have to fight more than the cold.

"How many cartridges do we have left?" I finally asked.

"Enough to do some damage," Crenshaw said, running his fingers around his gun belt. "I've got maybe thirty, counting the handful I dropped in my pocket."

I had done no shooting, and my belt loops still held about twenty-five .44-40 cartridges, which were interchangeable with the Winchesters.

"Only six left here," Kerlin said.

"I don't think there's much point in posting a sentry," Tom Crenshaw mused, puffing on his briar and glancing off into the darkness. "No moon tonight. Blacker than the inside of a boot. What few stars there are overhead won't help much."

"The sneaky devil will have just as much trouble seeing in the dark as we will," the Irishman said.

"Not if he settled into a good hiding place before dark and can see our camp fire. As much as I hate to say it, we'll have to let that fire die down or spend the night away from it."

"My God, man, we'll freeze to death," Kerlin objected.

"Whoever's out there isn't superhuman," I replied. "He probably won't have a fire, either. But he'll have all the advantage if we show a light."

"For the last half mile there hasn't been much of anyplace a sniper could hole up," Crenshaw said, raking the pipe stem thoughtfully across his stubbly chin. "The canyon walls are almost straight up and down here, so I know he couldn't have climbed out to get at us from above. And he didn't pass us. So any shots will have to come from that way." He pointed directly up canyon. "If one of us goes back up the trail to the next bend, we'll have him blocked from getting a shot at our camp."

"Provided he's not already closer than that, and one of us gets ambushed on the trail in the dark," I said.

"I've an idea, lads," Kerlin offered. "Why not let our fire die down and then make our way on downriver another furlong or so and bed down. It'll be colder than the stare of a British officer, but we can sleep huddled together while our friend watches the glow of our fire the rest of the night."

"That sounds like the best suggestion yet." Crenshaw nodded. "Let our talk and our fire die down gradually and then we'll ease out. We'll have to take turns carrying Chavez. And, for God's sake, be careful. We'll be feeling our way. So go slow and quiet. One slip will give the whole thing away, the way noise echoes in this place. Besides that, I don't want any of us falling into this damn river. The noise of that rushing water should cover any small sounds we make."

In a short time the whole thing was accomplished. Diego Chavez mumbled softly in his sleep as the muscular Crenshaw scooped him up and carried him as one would a baby. But the wounded man never came fully awake. We were casual about it, talking to each other as if we were just settling in for the night, not knowing if our voices were echoing the erroneous message to some unseen gunman a few hundred yards away in the darkness. We slid off into the darkness one at a time, met a short distance away and Kerlin took the lead with Crenshaw second, carrying Chavez. We crept along close to the splintered granite wall, stepping cautiously to avoid the uneven spots, and staying as far from the sound of the river as we could.

When I judged we had covered two hundred yards, Kerlin stopped where a small outcropping seemed to shut off the wind. Crenshaw put down his burden with a grunt of relief, and we proceeded to huddle as close as we could for warmth, the wounded man between us, covered with all the clothes and blankets we had.

But it was a restless night at best. I dozed off and on, from sheer exhaustion, but the others were also tossing and turning. Sleeping on bare, rocky, frozen ground was next to impossible. But finally I fell into a fairly sound sleep about two hours before daylight. The cold drove Kerlin out early, and the rest of us joined him as the early gray light filtered down into the canyon, showing a ragged slice of pale sky overhead. All of us were stiff and sore and bleary-eyed. Chavez's wound looked good and had bled no more, but his whole left side was very stiff and painful.

Some cold drinks of water, and we were on our way. By the time the sun was fully up, we had worked ourselves fairly warm. Even Chavez was walking reasonably well on his makeshift blanket boots. Whatever pain he was feeling never brought a whimper or whine or complaint from his lips. He might have been out for a Sunday stroll in the park.

We had covered several miles by the time we paused to rest. The sun was reaching its zenith and was slanting its warmest rays of the day obliquely into the chasm.

It was while we were standing still, with two of us sitting on the ground, resting, that our stalker hit us again. The crack of the rifle and the slug slamming off the rock wall came almost simultaneously. We dove for some small rocks at the base of the wall, bringing up our rifles and dragging Chavez with us at the same time.

"Where is he?"

"Didn't see the puff." Nothing was visible to our probing eyes — no telltale movement, no sound, no second shot.

"You okay?" I looked over at Crenshaw who was jammed against me as we tried to make ourselves smaller than we were. He nodded, and I saw some trickles of blood running down his cheek. "Some chips of rock got me."

"By damn, he's a persistent devil!" Kerlin said from behind me where he lay prone, with Chavez flattened against the wall beside him.

"You think he's really trying to kill us, or is he just trying to come close and scare the hell out of us?"

"He has to be an expert shot to come as close as he has come intentionally without meaning to hit us," Crenshaw said, smearing the blood on his face with a quick swipe of his left hand.

"Don't do anything stupid," I warned, as I saw his ears reddening. He had lost his hat in his dive for cover, and the wind was stirring his black hair. "I hope he can't see us here, or he can pick us off with ease. We got to do something. We can't stay here."

"He may be waiting for us to come out into his line of fire again."

Crenshaw glanced up and down at the big splinters of rock that were partially sheltering us. The rock wall here looked terraced, tilting up and back in a series of about three broken, uneven ledges. It was too steep to climb, but the boulders that had broken off to form these ledges lay in a scattered jumble along the base of the granite wall and on the edge of the river. The rock that still clung to the wall and formed the two rough terraces was seamed and split everywhere and, in the natural course of geologic action, would eventually break off and come tumbling down.

"Have you still got that black powder?" Crenshaw asked.

"Right here under my coat."

"Let's use it to slow this guy down or stop him altogether. Think you can wiggle over and plant it in that seam of rock?"

He pointed at a long sliver of black, vertical shadow that marked the seam between a huge slab of rock and the wall. I wouldn't have to expose myself to set the charge. I worked the packet out of my coat and unwound the four-foot length of fuse that was wrapped around it.

"Throw a few shots up that way to keep him occupied."

Crenshaw jacked a round into the chamber, aimed in the general direction of our attacker, and the rifle jerked and crashed.

I crouched and sprang, clutching the cumbersome packet. The rock seam was about ten yards in front and to my left. It was only a matter of a couple of minutes for me to attach the fuse and then find a portion of the crack large enough to shove the packet into. I wedged it back inside to the length of my arm, stringing the fuse until it began to sputter. As soon as

Crenshaw saw it start to smoke, his rifle spoke up with a roar.

As I leapt back down the canyon, Mike Kerlin had Chavez draped over his shoulder and was literally running with him over the broken ledge of rock, slipping dangerously on the sun-softened snow. I was right on his heels. Then the slamming of the rifle blasts receded in echoes as Crenshaw followed us.

More distant shots rang out, and something lifted my hat from my head, sending it sailing into the surging river.

We had run little more than a hundred yards when a rumble shook the ground, and then a concussion of sound slammed my ears, and we stumbled forward into the ground as the crashing, roaring sound followed us and rolled over us, echoing and reechoing.

From the ground I twisted around with my ears ringing and saw the narrow canyon filled with a cloud of smoke and dust. I could still hear rocks cascading from the wall and filling the narrow trail and splashing into the river. It seemed an eternity before the crashing and the pattering of small stones ceased and the wind began to shred the veil of smoke and dust. The trail behind us was completely blocked with tons of granite boulders and slabs of all sizes and shapes piled together. Part of the river was also filled with the shattered pieces of the rock wall. If our gunman wasn't buried under that rockfall, at least he had been cut off and silenced by it.

We gathered ourselves up and set off again, confident that unless our sniper could somehow find a way to fly like a hawk to the canyon rim far above, he would not be able to pursue us any farther.

"Lucky we didn't plug the river with that blast," I commented.

"Right you are about that," Crenshaw agreed. "That water would've backed up behind that rockfall. When she came over the top or busted through, she'd o' come arippin'. And us with no place to go to avoid it."

Diego Chavez seemed to have recovered some energy and was moving well on his blanket-wrapped feet and legs. Even so, it was after four o'clock and graying toward dusk when we finally reached end-of-track at Canon City and gratefully piled aboard our handcar for the trip back to Pueblo. There would be no warm caboose to ride in on the way back, but the grade was gradually downhill. Even though we had to pump the handles, it wasn't bad once we got up our momentum and went whizzing along with the wind whipping in our faces. In any event, it was a great relief not to be walking. And I'm sure the others felt the same, especially Chavez.

It was just after eight o'clock when we finally rolled into our camp at Pueblo. Crenshaw reported directly to the road's chief engineer, Joel McManus, while Kerlin and I got Chavez some clothes before hunting up the only doctor in Pueblo.

Dr. Edward Burchfield was a vigorous man in his late forties who operated out of an office in the back of his home in Pueblo. He had not yet gone to bed when we pulled up in our borrowed buckboard and rapped at his door. His wife answered and showed us into the office while she called her husband.

We briefly explained what had happened as Chavez pulled off his coat and shirt.

"You say this happened yesterday?" the doctor asked, pressing gently around the ugly, clogged hole. Chavez never blinked an eye.

"Good thing you got here when you did; it was about to become infected. Lie down on this table."

It was only a matter of minutes for him to boil some instruments.

"This is going to hurt. Do you want something for pain?"

Chavez shook his head.

"Maybe a shot of whiskey, then?" Dr. Burchfield asked.

Again Chavez declined.

"You boys may want to hold him down so he doesn't jump at the wrong time."

Kerlin and I placed ourselves at his head and his feet.

"Ready?" the doctor asked.

Chavez nodded slightly.

The instrument began to probe and I could feel the patient's body stiffen as I held his ankles. Silence reigned for the next minute or two, with only the sound of breathing. Sweat poured off Diego's face, and his jaw muscles bulged as he gritted his teeth. The doctor directed Kerlin to turn up the wick on the overhead coal-oil lamp.

I was almost hoping Chavez would pass out, but his black eyes continued to stare at the ceiling.

At last Dr. Burchfield straightened up, with the deformed lump of lead held in the bloody forceps.

"A piece of cloth was driven in there with it," he commented as he dropped the bullet on a towel and began cleaning and disinfecting the wound.

After the wound was bandaged and Chavez mopped off, dressed, and back on his feet, Kerlin helped him outside to the buckboard while I hung back to pay the doctor.

"Sure appreciate it, Doc," I said, handing him some greenbacks.

"Glad to help," he replied.

We walked out onto the front porch, the yellow light from the doorway streaming out around us in the frosty air.

"By the way, Dr Burchfield," I said, pausing and glancing back at the buckboard, "did you happen to notice the scars on that man's back?"

"Yes."

"Have you any idea what caused them?"

"Where's that man from?" He answered my

question with a question.

"Some miles south of here. A village in the mountains of the northern New Mexico Territory. Why?"

"He's obviously of Spanish or Mexican descent. Catholic, I presume."

I shrugged. "I don't know much about him." I couldn't imagine what this had to do with my question.

"I think I could hazard a guess about those scars."

I waited.

"Those three vertical and three horizontal gashes are the mark of initiation into Los Hermanos Penitentes."

"The what?"

"The Penitent Brothers. An order of Catholic laymen who practice severe religious bodily penance, especially during Lent. The Church frowns on their rigorous punishments, so they've pretty much gone underground in recent years. But the organization is still flourishing in many villages and rural areas of Colorado and northern New Mexico. It has something to do with their Hispanic heritage, I believe."

"Let's go, Matt! It's getting cold out here!" Mike Kerlin called.

I hesitated, wanting to question him further. But the doctor, standing there in his shirtsleeves, was obviously anxious to get back inside. So I just thanked him again and left.

As I climbed onto the seat of the buckboard, I glanced back at the blanket-wrapped figure reclining behind us. My curiosity was whetted. What lay behind the somber black eyes of Diego Chavez? What sort of religious order or cult was this the doctor had hinted at? I made a mental note to find out more about Los Hermanos Penitentes.

Chapter 7

April came in with definite signs of an early spring on the high plains. It also came in with definite signs of a hotter war between the Denver & Rio Grande Railroad and the Atchison, Topeka and Santa Fe Railroad. After our encounter with the unseen sniper three and a half weeks earlier, General Palmer ordered Joel McManus, his head man in the field, to send larger armed patrols into the Gorge. These armed patrols were to harass any work crews they found. Other groups of armed men, equipped to stay in the field for a week or two at a time, were sent overland by horseback around the rim of the canyon to head off any further road building by the Santa Fe beyond Royal Gorge toward Leadville. With the snow melt and the coming of warmer weather, both sides were determined to strengthen their respective positions to this vital right-of-way into the mountains.

But still the Supreme Court dragged its judicial feet. No decision was forthcoming. If no judgment was rendered soon, I was very much afraid that this conflict would erupt into open warfare, and lawsuits be damned. Both General Palmer and the head of the Santa Fe were men determined to have their way, regardless of the niceties of the law. They were men used to taking the bull by the horns and making things happen. Had they been the timid types, they probably would have stayed out of railroading altogether.

"Wanta ride up front with me?" Gregory DeArmand asked as the panting steam engine stood on the siding near our boxcar encampment, ready to pull out for Denver.

I was glad for the invitation since the prospect of riding all the way to Denver in a boxcar with a half dozen other laborers, half of whom I hardly knew, didn't particularly appeal to me. Kerlin, Chavez, and Crenshaw were there, however. The train consisted of engine, tender, five loaded coal cars, three empty boxcars, and a caboose. We were to deliver the coal to Denver, and load up bags of grain, foodstuffs, farm tools, boots, and clothing for the return trip. Gregory DeArmand, the big stoker who I had first met at Colorado Springs on my way south in February, had drawn this run, and I was more than happy to accept his invitation to ride the cab with him. He would keep me entertained all the way.

"Actually, I have another motive besides just your company for having you up front." He grinned as I picked up my bedroll and followed him through the quagmire of mud toward the head of the train.

"What's that?"

"You can use the coal pick and break up those big lumps for me."

"Sure." This still beat riding the boxcar. In fact, I was really thrilled to be invited to share the cab of one of these beautiful locomotives. The Poncha was a fairly new engine, having been recently delivered from the Baldwin Locomotive Works in Pennsylvania. Its gleaming black sheet metal and polished brass comprised a machine that, to me, had always meant the epitome of sleek beauty, speed, and power. I had admired locomotives since my childhood. Since we weren't pulling any mountain grades on this run, an extra locomotive was not needed. The Poncha was an eight-wheeler, including a pair of pony trucks in front. Its drive wheels were thirty-six inches in diameter. It had a diamond-shaped stack and roomy cab and weighed about forty thousand pounds.

"Gil, this here's Matt Tierney. He'll be riding the deck with us."

The engineer shifted the long-spout oil can to his left hand and I met his grip. Gilbert Latham was a tall, lean, taciturn man, friendly in a quiet sort of way, I was to discover later. He was also a diehard D&RG man, one of many skilled employees who had been kept on when the line was leased to the Santa Fe.

"Weren't you involved in that little fracas up the Gorge a few weeks back?"

I nodded. "Yup."

He chuckled. "Wish I'da been there to see the look on that sniper's face when that black powder went off. Welcome aboard."

"Thanks."

A few minutes later Gil climbed up and slid into his leather seat at the right side of the cab. I climbed up and deposited myself on the coal pile in the tender, where I was well out of the way, but could see down into the cab, which seemed filled with knobs, handles, gauges, and levers between the two tall, narrow windows that looked forward along each side of the engine.

DeArmand followed me in, swinging his huge frame gracefully up on the hand rods. He grinned at me and rolled up the sleeves of his blue wool shirt and prepared to go to work. He had laid his fire earlier, and steam pressure was up in the boiler. It was now a matter of maintaining that pressure as the engineer used it. He wiped down the boiler jacket with a cotton rag. The safety valves sang a thin, high-pitched wail against full pressure. Lazy smoke curled from the squat stack.

On a signal from the brakeman, Gil Latham gave two short blasts of the whistle by way of an overhead cord and released his driver brakes. Leaning his head and shoulders out the side window, he gradually opened the throttle handle with his left hand, feeding steam into the cylinders. From the stack came a muffled *whoof!,* followed by another and then another as the Poncha gathered herself for the long pull to Denver.

I handed DeArmand his big scoop shovel, which had been rounded off on the corners for ease of handling.

"Use that pick back there to break up some of these larger hunks," DeArmand said, nodding at the coal pile I rested on. "Here's about the size I need." He slid his scoop smoothly into the pile and then pivoted. The fire door clanged open, and he scattered the coal inside the blazing opening with a deft movement, slamming the door shut again.

Even with a load behind her, the little Baldwin was a smooth, fast machine, I discovered within the space of a few miles. I guessed we were rolling at more than fifty miles per hour, and she seemed to be loafing. The gentle swells of the prairie were no challenge as we rocked along, swaying from side to side with the fresh April breeze whipping around the back of the open cab. My labors with the pick and the continuous burps of heat from the opening and closing fire door assured that I would not get chilly from the early morning wind. I didn't overwork myself. I left plenty of time to enjoy the springlike weather, with a view of the mountains sliding past on our left. It was a unique privilege to be riding the cab of a beautiful new locomotive that responded like a thing alive to the touch of the engineer and fireman. It was exhilarating to smell the aroma of burning coal, hot valve oil, and steam. I could hear the slight pounding of the side rods driving us.

At length, DeArmand stuck his shovel into the pile I had pulled down close for him. He leaned back on his seat box, wiping the sweat from his face with a sleeve.

"Wanta give 'er a try?" he asked, gesturing at the firebox.

"Me?"

"Sure. Why not? Any objections, Gil?"

The engineer shook his head. "Nope. Not as long as we don't lose *too* much pressure."

I gladly laid aside the small pick I had been using and pulled his shovel out of the pile. I had been watching him for several miles, and he seemed to have a method of firing that was both efficient for the engine and labor-saving for the stoker. I had no hope of duplicating it, but I was eager to try.

"She carries one hundred and sixty pounds of steam," he was saying. "And you're in for a treat, whether you know it or not. This baby is one of the sweetest engines you'll ever see. Smooth and strong, with no bad characteristics I've seen since I first fired her."

He yanked the fire door open with a chain. "There ya go. Give 'er a couple o' scoops."

I did as he directed, the scoop clanging clumsily against the opening.

"Sling the next one in so it scatters around a little."

I attempted to follow his directions, but shovel as I might, in less than a mile we were losing pressure so badly he had to cut down on the flow of water to the boiler.

I handed the scoop back to DeArmand. He smoothed his big, black mustache with one hand and grinned slightly. "Nothing to it. Now watch what I do." He dug the scoop into the coal.

"First of all," he said, swinging around, "I start with a fire that's well built and level. This baby's a free steamer with perfect drafting, so what I'm about to show you's easy. It's not so easy on other locomotives. Now, once I get this built back up, I'll show you." He worked until the steam pressure was back up to one hundred and sixty on the gauge.

"Now watch. I scatter one scoop of coal along the right-hand sheet, a second along the left-hand side, and then slap the third against the fire ring, so it fans out over the center and under the door. A light fire, a level fire, and a bright fire with a minimum of smoke makes for the greatest efficiency. And," he added with a wink at me, "it's a helluva lot easier on the fireman, too."

Gilbert Latham had been watching us closely. Finally, he could stand it no longer.

"Here, let me try that." He slid his long legs off the seat and reached for the scoop. But his efforts were no more successful than mine had been.

"Damn, DeArmand, didn't mean to mess up your fire. But it looked so easy!" He resumed his right-hand seat.

I had the feeling the big stoker was having fun at our expense and showing off a little, but I didn't mind. It was a totally new experience for me, and I was learning.

A short time later Gil pinched off some steam and we slowed.

"What's the matter?" I asked, sticking my head out of the left side window. About a half mile ahead, a dozen or so tawny pronghorn antelope were bounding across the right-of-way in long, graceful leaps. Latham pulled the overhead cord and a long, wavering blast of sound burst from the steam whistle.

"Won't be much longer, we'll have to be watchin' out for herds o' cattle on the tracks," Latham remarked, easing the throttle open again, "the way new ranchers are coming into this region and building up their herds. Not just homesteaders, either. Lots of outside backers and investors, I hear."

A short time later Latham began slowing as we approached the depot at Colorado Springs.

"We'll stop here for about forty-five minutes for an early lunch," he announced, pulling out his watch and glancing at it.

The train slowed even more and finally ground to a halt at the depot platform.

"Let's eat at the hotel. It's only a half block from here," DeArmand suggested, swinging his bulk down from the cab. I followed him and soon found that the hotel he referred to was the very same one where I had met him and the fight had occurred several weeks before. "Good food and fast service," he said, when I remarked about this.

I soon found out why he preferred the hotel after I had polished off a delicious lunch of broiled mountain trout and fried potatoes.

The brakeman and the other men riding in the boxcar were also eating at the hotel.

When we ambled back to our train, pleasantly stuffed and picking our teeth, we found Gil Latham leaning against the cab, a strange look on his face.

"What's up?" DeArmand asked.

"Just got a message over the wire from Denver that there's been a washout ahead, and we're being sidetracked here until it's repaired."

"Damn!"

"Did they say how long?" I asked.

"Nope. Could be a few hours, or even a day or so."

"I guess the spring runoff musta done it."

"Maybe." Gil Latham looked dubious. "Wish I could take a run up the line and look for myself."

"Why's that?" I inquired.

" 'Cause I don't halfway believe that message. Ever since the higher-ups operatin' this road are doing everything in their power to ruin this line. Mostly it's legal, like charging outrageous freight rates and passenger fares to drive off business. And arranging phony delays for all kinds of trumped-up reasons so we can't stay on schedule. I'm mighty suspicious that this so-called washout is just another delaying tactic to keep us from delivering this coal on time and picking up our return freights." He pulled off his gloves and slapped them against his thigh. "The message didn't say exactly where the washout was, but I'd lay this month's wages on the bet that there isn't one. I just came down from Denver a couple of days ago, and the roadbed was fine."

"All that melted snow in the mountains could've done some damage in a hurry," DeArmand observed. "It's possible."

"I know. I know." Gil snorted, climbing into the cab. "Let's get this thing on a siding and pass the word back to the other men."

This enforced delay was no personal concern of mine, even though DeArmand and the engineer seemed very irritated about it. While he kept periodic watch on his boiler fire, the rest of us laborers whiled away several hours in the billiard room of the hotel. Kerlin was one of the half dozen or so men who had been riding in the boxcar, and, over a game of pool, I regaled him with the tale of my experiences as a fireman.

"Aye. Sounds as if you mayn't have the touch for that," the big Irishman remarked, leaning over the table for a shot.

"Maybe with a little practice, I could get the hang of it," I said. "Even the engineer couldn't keep the steam pressure up. It looks a lot easier than it is."

"That's the way of it with many things," he answered, grimacing at the missed shot as his ball bounced off the rail.

I laughed, chalking my cue.

"Señor Matt . . ."

I looked around to see Diego Chavez standing near the table.

"Hi, Diego. How's the shoulder? Didn't think the foreman would be lettin' you come on a work run like this so soon."

"Oh, the shoulder is okay. Only a little stiff in the mornings." He rotated his arm to show us its flexibility.

"Want to get in a game with us?"

"No. *Gracias.*"

I leaned over and took my shot, and missed. Diego stood there hesitantly, as if he wanted to ask something further, rather than just watching us play.

"Why the long face?" I grinned at him. "You want a beer? I'm buying."

Again he shook his head.

"How long will we be here?" he finally asked.

I shrugged. "Don't know. The engineer said it could be a few hours or it might be sometime tomorrow before we can move on. Depends on how long it takes a work crew to fix that washout."

"Matt, you have been my friend, and I want to ask a favor." He seemed embarrassed to continue.

"Sure. What is it?"

"I need to go home."

"Home? You mean back to Pueblo? Are you sick?"

"No. To my village. You see" — he spread his hands in a pleading gesture — "Holy Week is coming very soon. I must return to my village for the services. It is *muy importante.* I am gone the whole season of Lent. But I must return for the Holy Week services to my village in New Mexico."

"Just ask the foreman for some time off," I suggested.

"Ah, but I have been off for more than three weeks, since my shoulder was shot," he said. "I am just now returning to work. Señor Crenshaw says I am fit for duty. I already ask him. I cannot quit. I need this job."

I glanced across the room to where Tom Crenshaw was leaning on the bar and sipping a beer. "Turned ya down, did he? Did you tell him why you wanted off?"

Chavez nodded.

"Even if he let you go, how would you get there? Can't catch the cars south 'cause they're cut off by the washout north of here."

"I have some money. I will rent a horse."

"You must want to get to New Mexico very badly," Kerlin said.

"*Sí.* It is most important that I go now. That is why I ask this favor of you, to plead with Señor Crenshaw for me. You know him. He favors both of you. If you ask him, he will let me go."

When I looked dubious, he hurried on. "I am not strong, not good yet for much work beside these other hombres. You can tell him my wound still pains me."

"Does it?"

"*Sí*. Sometimes."

"If you have to go home for some religious ceremonies, you shouldn't have volunteered to come on this work detail."

"The foreman ordered me to come."

"Okay, I'll talk to him." I laid down my cue. "Where's your village?"

"San Jose. It is north and west of Taos. By riding steadily I can be there Sunday."

I started toward Crenshaw.

"*Gracias, señor.* My brothers are expecting me."

"You come from a large family?" Kerlin asked.

"No. These *hermanos* are not of my family." He did not elaborate.

I approached Crenshaw, spoke a few pleasant words, and sized up his mood. It seemed pleasant enough, and I drew him slightly to one side and explained what I wanted. "He's probably not strong enough yet to do much work. And this is really important to him."

The short, stocky foreman shook his head. "Damned if I know why this Mexican ever hired on with us. If I let him go, he won't be back for at least two weeks."

"Well, he won't be getting paid for it, will he?"

"No."

"Then what's the harm? That shoulder's healed, but I don't think he's really strong enough to do much yet. It will give him more time to recuperate."

"I suppose he'll want to draw his pay before he goes," he growled.

"He didn't mention it. If he doesn't come back at all, the company will have saved that much of his pay."

"Well, okay. I guess he won't be much help to us at that. Tell him to go on." He waved me off and went back to his beer.

I relayed the news to Diego. His handsome face lit up in a toothy smile. "I knew you could do it, Matt," he enthused, pumping my hand.

"Nothing to it. As one gringo to another, I told him you wouldn't draw your pay before you left."

I expected him to balk at this, but he just kept grinning and pumping my hand. "You are my friend. I will not forget you for this. I will return in about ten days, God willing."

"What's so important that you'll miss a week and a half of pay?" Kerlin wanted to know.

"You would not understand. It is part of my religion. Very important."

"I'm a Catholic, too. I've been to Holy Week services. But they weren't something I couldn't miss."

"It is different with my people, señor. My brothers are expecting me. *Gracias!*"

He waved as he left the room and headed for the livery stable.

"That's the second time he has mentioned his brothers," Kerlin said, racking the balls for the next game.

"I think he's referring to his brothers in the fraternity," I said, thoughtfully.

"Fraternity?"

"A brotherhood. Los Hermanos Penitentes. The Penitent Brothers."

I had not confided in Kerlin earlier, but now I did, telling what little the doctor had told me about this semisecret organization.

Much to my surprise, Kerlin was keenly interested and wanted to know more.

"That's all I know about it," I said.

"I must see this for myself."

"What?"

"This is a once-in-a-lifetime opportunity. I have always been a man to seize opportunities. When I was in Natal and Zululand, I took every chance I had to learn more about the Zulus and their customs and dress and religion."

"But this is different. This is just a Christian Holy Week service."

"Christian, is it?" He snorted. "Holy Mother preserve us. You call lashing yourself with a cactus whip a Christian ceremony?"

"Keep your voice down," I said, glancing around. "Not everyone knows about this."

He seemed to have lost all interest in our game as he laid his cue across the table.

"What's not Christian about it? They're just imitating the scourging Christ suffered."

"It's barbaric," Kerlin stated flatly. "There is nothing in the Catholic religion that says that kind of thing is encouraged or even allowed. Even the heathen Zulu tribesmen wouldn't do such a thing."

I shrugged. "Maybe that's why the Catholic Church has been trying to stop it — and driven them into hiding."

As I talked, Mike was reaching for his coat, which hung on a wall peg nearby.

"Where are you going?"

"I told you I absolutely must see this ceremony. If it is to be believed, I must see it with my own eyes."

"How do you aim to do that?"

"I'm going to follow him. What did you say the name of that village was?"

"San Jose. But you can't just walk out. Are you quitting your job?"

"Ah, yes, the job. I must think of some way around that." He paused a moment, coat in hand.

"Tell you what. If you go, I'm going with you. If this train gets out of here in the next few hours, we'll be in Denver and back to Pueblo in about forty-eight hours. We'd still have time to take a few days off and get the passenger cars south on toward Raton Pass. We could rent a wagon or a couple of horses at Uncle Billy Wooten's place and ride on down to San Jose by Monday or Tuesday."

He looked dubious, as if I were trying to maneuver him out of going.

"Think so?"

"Sure. Crenshaw would never rehire us if we walked out on him now in the midst of this run to Denver. But when we get back . . . well, that's a different story. Laborers are always coming and going in the D and RG camp. Even though General Palmer has the reputation for being a wheeler-dealer and a free spender, the men under him are sure not averse to saving a few bucks when they can, and that includes not having to pay us five dollars per day each for a week or so if there's nothing much for us to do. There won't be any problem getting hired back in a week or two as the spring comes on. Things seem to be working toward a showdown with the Santa Fe. They'll need us. What do you say? The more I think about it, the more I think I'd like to take a peek at those Penitentes myself."

"What you say makes good sense, but what if we are sidetracked here for a day or more?"

I shrugged. "Let's cross that bridge if and when we come to it. If we pull out of here for Denver by noon tomorrow, we should make it with time to spare. If it appears we're going to be delayed, we'll just play it by ear and do whatever it takes to get there. Don't worry. Loosen up. You're still too regimented. You're not in Her Majesty's army now. This is America."

He grinned and looped his coat back over the peg. "Right you are."

"One thing we have to be thinking about," I

said as I led him out of the billiard room toward the dining room.

"And what might that be?"

"We have to find somebody who's on the inside. Some native who speaks fluent Spanish, who knows the Penitentes, and who is willing to help us get close enough to observe them."

"My Irish friend, you have just spoken a mouthful. Where will we ever find such a person? He, in effect, would be a traitor to his own people. Such men must be rare."

"You forget that you are in a new country where anything is possible."

"That's what the British thought in Zululand."

Word came over the wire at ten o'clock the next morning that the washout had been repaired. DeArmand built up his banked fire. Shortly after eleven, with the steam gauges pointing at maximum pressure, Gil Latham gave two blasts on the whistle and eased the throttle open. Our big drive wheels dug in, and we slowly began moving toward the open switch that led to the main line and Denver.

The engineer didn't appear upset over the twenty-four-hour delay. When I mentioned it, he just shrugged from his window seat and told me that ever since General Palmer had been forced to lease the D&RG to his rival road, it had been this way. Poor maintenance on equipment, worn-out equipment not replaced, resulting in many minor and at least two major accidents. Some of the D&RG employees had resigned and gone looking for other work when they saw how dangerous working conditions had become.

"Damn shame, too," Latham said. "This

could be a mighty fine and profitable road if the big shots would just quit fightin' and agree on where each of 'em was gonna run. Greed's gonna be the downfall of this country yet." He spat out the open window into the April breeze. "It's a cinch the Santa Fe management is out to ruin this line while it's in their control, so if General Palmer ever does get it back, he'll have to sell off what's left to pay off the bond holders and break even. And, unless I miss my guess, the Santa Fe will be right there to gobble up whatever's bein' sold."

"Why don't you jump off before this whole thing comes crashing down?" I asked.

"Reckon I should," he replied slowly. "But I don't aim to let a friend down when he needs me. General Palmer gave me my start a few years back, and I ain't likely to forget that. Besides, I really admire the man. He's got spunk. He'll take on anybody, and he's smart to boot. I'm gonna stick around and see this thing through. If the D and RG collapses, there'll be time enough to look for other work."

I nodded. I wondered if this General Palmer knew just what kind of loyal employees he had. If they were all as good as the two I shared this cab with, he would still stand a good chance of saving his line.

DeArmand got his rhythm of three-scoops-and-rest that he had tried to show me the day before, and we were rolling along smoothly. I could smell the acrid coal smoke blowing back from the stack and could hear the wheels clicking over the joints in the rails.

"Just what is the advantage of a narrow gauge over the standard gauge?" I asked as DeArmand clanged the fire door shut and leaned back on his window seat.

"Cheaper construction costs," he replied, folding his arms across his chest. "Especially in the mountains. Don't have to grade such a wide roadway. Ties don't have to be as long. A lot less metal goes into the rails, since they are not as tall as standard, and they weigh only thirty pounds per foot. Standard rails weigh about twice that."

I nodded. "Seems like it wouldn't make a wide enough footing to be stable."

"Doesn't seem to present any problem. The locomotives and cars are built for it. I guess the engineers have got it all figured out. I don't know of any derailments that have been caused by the narrowness of the tracks."

As DeArmand picked up his shovel and went back to work, I retrieved my small pick and started breaking up the larger lumps of coal I was sitting on. I was afraid Kerlin might be offended that he had not been invited to ride up front in the cab, but he just grinned and said he would much rather be playing poker with the boys in the boxcar than breaking up coal with me.

As I picked the black chunks of anthracite, I thought of Chavez. How far south was he by now? I was sure if he stopped to sleep last night, it was only briefly and then more to rest the horse than himself. He was, even now, streaking south toward Raton Pass on a fast horse, the urge to take part in a centuries-old rite pushing him on.

"So you come here asking me about Los Hermanos Penitentes?" Juan Jaramillo strode to the cherry sideboard and selected a slim cigar from a humidor. His tone was sharp and guarded. Without offering me or Kerlin a cigar, he struck a match and lit his smoke. Then he turned and regarded us across the room of his elegantly furnished Denver home.

"If you had not been sent here by my old friend and *compadre*, Gilbert Latham, I would ask my servant to show you out immediately. However, you are guests in my house for now. Please be seated," he added in a somewhat gentler tone, waving us toward the horsehair furniture. In spite of his obvious irritation, the innate Hispanic courtesy and formal hospitality came to the fore.

Juan Jaramillo was well into middle age, but his hair was still black as a jackdaw's wing, as Kerlin later described it. His dark skin and somewhat thick nose hinted at a trace of Indian blood in his ancestral past, but his aristocratic bearing was every bit the Castilian Spanish that his name implied. He was a self-made man, Latham had told me — a man he had met years before as a laborer on the Union Pacific Railroad. He had become successful in the cattle business on the eastern slopes of the Rockies and later diversified, investing some of his profits in a Denver dry goods store. While not fabulously wealthy, he was financially well-fixed for life, barring some calamity.

Since we had arrived more than a day later than scheduled in Denver, we had been delayed in unloading our coal, and Latham had directed us to Juan Jaramillo as the best source he knew of for information on the Penitentes.

"Why are you interested in the brotherhood?" Jaramillo asked when we were seated. He remained standing, leaning on the sideboard.

I dared not confess that I was motivated by morbid curiosity, but when neither of us replied immediately, I think he read our thoughts. Especially, I dared not let him know that I was a former newspaper reporter and was still a free-lance writer.

"I suspected as much," he went on, almost with a sneer. "You two are the types who would be in the front row at a hanging, or to view the mutilated corpses at an Apache massacre, or to watch a bullfight, hoping the matador would be gored. I have no patience with your kind. You may relax in my house as long as you wish, but I see no reason to give you any information about the Penitentes."

I was suddenly very conscious of the coal

dust on my work clothes, and the fair skin and hair and strange brogue of Kerlin — both of us very much two outlanders, worlds removed from the secret Spanish society we had come asking about. I suspected that this man's confidence had been violated in the past by just such gringos as the two of us.

His hard black eyes rested on us, waiting for us to speak.

"We are both Catholics," I finally blurted out, feeling the need to establish some rapport with this man. "Mr. Kerlin, here, is from Ireland, but has spent several years in the British Army in various parts of the world. I was born in Ireland and came to this country with my parents when I was only a child. Both of us have been reared in the faith and its ancient traditions. Recently we helped save the life of one of our fellow workers — a young man from a village in the mountains of New Mexico. It was shortly after that we discovered by accident that he was a member of the Penitent Brothers. As those who share the same faith in Christ, we naturally wanted to know more about this aspect of our own religion that we had never before encountered. It is for this reason that we are coming to ask you for a deeper explanation of practices that to the rest of the world must seem strange and barbaric.

Our host did not reply immediately. He looked from one to the other of us, as if trying to discern our true motives.

"How much did this fellow worker of yours tell you?" he finally asked.

"Nothing, really. What little I know was provided by a doctor who treated his wound. I was curious about the scars on my friend's back. And two days ago I persuaded our foreman to let Diego leave his job for a couple of weeks to return to his village for Holy Week."

Juan Jaramillo nodded, apparently satisfied that we were not the sensation seekers he had first suspected.

"Because there is so much misinformation about the brotherhood, I will tell you exactly what it is all about. Would you care for a cigar, or something to drink, perhaps?"

We both declined. Jaramillo seated himself in an armchair opposite us and crossed his legs as he began to talk. The afternoon sun flooded in the front window past the drapes that had been drawn aside with heavy cords. Motes of dust drifted lazily in the shafts of sunlight as the older man sat silently, his furrowed face a study in concentration as he arranged his thoughts.

"The fraternity has ancient roots, going back to the earliest centuries after Christ. In fact, the practice of self-flagellation was known among the ancient Greeks, who appeased their pagan gods in this manner. The practice of corporal penance really came to the fore in harsher times in Europe, during the Middle Ages, from about 1200 onward. Saint Anthony of Padua was one of the first to found a fraternity that included public self-whipping as part of religious observance. The practice spread and was especially used as public penance around outbreaks of the Black Death. History tells us of processions, on religious holy days and during Lent and Holy Week, of devout Christians carrying crosses, dragging chains, and flagellating themselves with leather whips. This was not at all uncommon on the European continent. But it never took hold in England, for some reason. Two of the Popes in the 1300s and 1400s came out publicly against the practice, and the Inquisition drove the remaining practitioners underground for a time.

"When our own river kingdom was first settled and the Pueblo Indians converted along the Rio Grande in New Mexico, Oñate brought the practice with him and his Spanish soldiers and monks from Mexico City in the late 1500s. Even Oñate himself, the leader of the expedition, did severe penance on Good Friday, 1598, while in the field with his troops.

"In 1680 the Indians revolted — I am ashamed to say it, at the oppressive treatment of my forebears — killed many Spanish settlers, desecrated the missions, and the remaining Spaniards had to flee south across the river beyond El Paso del Norte. It wasn't until twelve years later that the Spaniards came north to Santa Fe again and made peace with the Indians, converting the Pueblos again, and Spanish families again settled in haciendas along the long stretch of river in New Mexico."

He paused and knocked the ash from his cigar into a brass cuspidor on the floor near his chair.

"How do you know so much about this?" I asked, and immediately wished I hadn't when I saw the offended look on his face.

"I may be a self-made man, sir, as you Anglos say. But I am not uneducated. I have a degree of formal schooling. And, even if I had not, the most unlettered of our people are aware of their own history. Is it not so in Ireland?"

Kerlin nodded.

"Spoken history has been around much longer than written history. But to return . . . Spain, as a world power, rich with the wealth of the New World, began to decline during the last century. The crown could no longer support the many Franciscan missions that were so far from her borders. The friars and the Indians they had converted were left more and more to fend for themselves, which included staving off attacks of Apaches who had been driven into New Mexico by drought and famine. They raided the missions and the isolated haciendas for livestock and food. Being isolated as they were, many of the sons and daughters who chose to remain on this frontier intermarried with the peaceful, Christianized Pueblo Indians. Towns and villages gradually developed outside of the family haciendas and the settled towns of Santa Fe and the old pueblo of Taos."

I slid my watch out of my pocket and snapped open the case. "It's all very interesting, this history of the New Mexico Territory, sir, but we have only a limited time."

He threw me a frosty look. "You came here seeking information, and I am providing it in my own fashion. If you do not wish to hear more . . ."

"No. No. Go on," Kerlin said hurriedly.

"Very well. I'll shorten this and bring it to the point. You must realize that the Spanish mind is very different from other races and nationalities. Spaniards — especially those of earlier times — were prone to excesses of cruelty and depravity, but also to excesses of piety. And their piety was not a false thing. They realized that great weaknesses and great sins called for atonement equally as great. And even though Christ's death on the cross atoned for all of us, it still remained for us to do what we could to add our sufferings to His in reparation for the evil we had done. As you know, personal sins can be forgiven, but we must try to make amends — much like paying a debt to an old friend. Anyway, when the mission system gradually crumbled and the Franciscan Order recalled most of the friars who had been serving this vast territory, societies of devout laymen came forward to fill the gap. They could not say Mass or perform most of the sacraments, but they continued to conduct religious services as best they could. In addition, these men, these *hermanos* as they came to call themselves, performed many charitable deeds in the village. They were assisted and aided in this by the women of the town. They sought to emulate their Lord and Master, Jesus Christ. Even though they had been left leaderless by the Church, the tradition of many generations was strong, and they clung to their faith. Some of the isolated villages were still visited from time to time by itinerant priests from Santa Fe or one of the missions that was still active. The brothers practiced severe penance and self-whippings, mostly during Lent. These men knew — had been brought up with the idea — that life was short and difficult and that Señor Death was a frequent visitor to their villages. They knew they were not destined to live long in this world, so that it would be wise to prepare for the next by making atonement for their many failings and, at the same time, making themselves more pleasing in the sight of God by imitating the sufferings that His Divine Son endured for us. Do you understand?"

"Yes. But I was told the Church tried to restrict their activities."

"*Sí.* That is true. The bishops at Santa Fe this century have condemned the Penitentes for what they called extreme penances."

"Why?" I asked, although I thought I already knew the answer.

"As you know, our faith teaches that to kill oneself is the worst form of despairing of God's goodness and mercy. It is a sure way to condemn oneself to the fiery pit, if one is not totally insane at the time."

I nodded.

"Since your body, as well as your soul, was given to you by the Creator, it must not be abused. And the Church fathers looked upon mortifications of the Penitent Brothers as mutilation of the body."

"Even Saint Paul mentions beating his own body to bring it into subjection. And many of the early hermits practiced severe forms of self-denial and pain," I objected.

"I know. I am only telling you how the Bishops of Santa Fe have looked upon it." He got up and paced over to the sideboard, where he struck another match to the cigar that had gone cold. "I have turned this over in my mind many times during the years," he continued. "Like many things in life, pleasure as well as pain, it is a matter of degree, of balance, if you will. As I see it, one must walk a middle road, without excesses on either side." He raised his smoking cigar to emphasize his point. "*That* is something that is easier to say than to do. But that is only my opinion. And you did not come here to hear my opinion. You want facts, and I am doing my best to provide them. But, when speaking of the Penitentes, how can one confine himself to facts? One must deal in conjecture and guesses, in generations of tradition and centuries of teaching, and in races and individuals' interpretations of that teaching. How can you get inside the head of your friend Diego? What he intends to do is no less a fact than the fact that he rode south toward his village yesterday. But much is hidden, and our senses deceive us."

"Señor Jaramillo, you strike me as a man who has had more than a little formal schooling," I said.

He smiled thinly, taking one last puff of his cigar and grinding it out in an ashtray on the sideboard.

"Yes. I was graduated from the university in Mexico City," he admitted. "I even studied for the priesthood for a time, but then I found the ladies . . ." He shrugged. "I went to work instead. Eventually I married a lovely woman and, over the years, God has been good to me." He gestured at the room. "In material things as well as in other ways."

"We would very much like to see this Penitente rite," Kerlin said.

I held my breath, waiting for the answer.

"That would be impossible. Because of the Church's censure — even at one time excommunication of active Penitentes — they are very secretive about their rituals. They are even more so now that a few gringos, such as yourselves, have secretly spied upon certain *moradas* in the past."

"Even if we came, not to scoff but to observe?" I asked.

He shook his head. "I'm afraid not."

"What would happen if we went down to San Jose, anyway?" Kerlin wanted to know.

"San Jose? That's where your friend Diego went?"

"Yes."

"I know that village. Mine was only a few miles from there. I visited there many times in my youth. I had several friends who lived there. But I have not seen them in years. The people are poor . . . so poor. I try to help them when I can, but . . ." He shrugged helplessly. "I came back to my village for a time after my graduation from the university. But there was nothing there for me. I had to leave. I was no longer content with village life. Other worlds waited for me." He looked very sad.

"What's wrong, Señor Jaramillo? Do you think maybe you made the wrong choice by leaving?" I felt bold enough to ask.

He shook his head. "No. It's just that . . . I miss the closeness, the strong faith, the caring for one another, aside from just one's family. I miss the brotherhood, and the sense of belonging."

"The brotherhood?"

"Los Hermanos Penitentes. I was of their number."

He turned and pulled the tail of his white linen shirt from his dark trousers in one quick motion that bared the lower half of his back. In the slanting sunlight from the window I saw the crisscrossing of countless marks, old scar tissue showing faintly white against the darker skin. I didn't know what to say, so I held my tongue.

After we had gotten a good look, he stuffed his shirt in and turned back to us. "I only wish I could go back and join the men of my *morada* in my village this Holy Week. Many are the sins I need to atone for. Excesses of the flesh are the weakness of younger men; wealth, arrogance, power, and greed are the temptations of older men. Much time has passed. . . ." His voice trailed off and he stood staring at nothing.

Suddenly he turned back to us. "But I forget myself. Perhaps you would care for some wine before you go?"

"Por favor."

He poured three glasses of wine from a large decanter on the sideboard. "I hope you like Madeira. It's all I have in the house. My favorite."

I sipped it. "Delicious."

The black eyes of the older man regarded Kerlin and me over the top of his glass. "I can see by your faces that you still intend to pursue your friend Diego to San Jose."

I was startled by his observation. "Well . . ." I glanced at Kerlin. "Yes."

"It is madness. Two fair-skinned outsiders would be in grave physical danger if they were caught spying on the Penitentes. They can be very resentful of intrusion on their privacy."

"Even from someone of their own faith?"

"Yes."

"Then maybe the bishops were right in trying to ban them or regulate their activities."

"Perhaps. But these are simple people of the mountains and deserts. They are a people of strong faith and strong passions. Ah . . . what's the use? How can I explain to an Anglo mind the fervor or the depth of a Spaniard? The best I can hope to do is to show you."

"What?"

"I will take you there myself and show you."

I was bewildered.

"You were going to go anyway, were you not?"

I nodded.

"The only safe way for you to go is for me to take you. No gringo outsiders would be allowed there otherwise. You could get yourselves hurt, maybe even killed."

"But —"

"No arguments." He held up his hand. "I have decided."

Then he smiled thinly. "I will admit that my decision was not entirely selfless. I have been meaning to go back every Lent for years. This just gave me the excuse I needed." He drained his glass. "Now, shall we discuss the details of where and when to meet before you must get back to your train?"

It came faintly at first, rising and falling on the cold night breeze of the mountain canyon. The shrill notes of the *pito,* the homemade reed flute, sent a chill up my back and the hair rising on my neck. They were coming.

Mike Kerlin and I glanced at each other in the darkness, and pushed ourselves up off the stony ground to crouch expectantly behind the bushes that bordered the trail. The rising three-quarter moon was just edging over the bulk of the Sangre de Cristo Mountains to the east and beginning to cast its light down into the narrow defile.

It was Wednesday night of Holy Week, and the two of us were lying in wait for a procession of Penitentes who had disappeared into the mountains before nightfall and were now returning toward their *morada,* or meeting house, about a half mile from the village. This was a sneaky way to go about it, but Juan Jaramillo had assured us it was the only way, before Holy Thursday, to get a glimpse of them. I wished for the partial comfort of having the older man with us, but he had gone off to visit the people and kin of his own village after escorting us to San Jose in a rented buckboard. But we were still nominally under his protection, since he had introduced us to the Hermano Mayor of San Jose. This white-haired, withered old man, one José Sebastian, was an old friend of Jaramillo's. The Hermano Mayor, or head brother, of the San Jose Penitentes, reluctantly agreed to allow us the privilege of watching the Holy Thursday and Good Friday services, provided we stayed well back and out of the way, and as inconspicuous as possible. He told Jaramillo that he, José Sebastian, could not be responsible for our safety since many of the villagers were resentful of Anglos. This was especially so since some Anglo outsiders a few years ago had disrupted the services by trying to make the worshipers stand still for photographs. Sebastian hinted, through Jaramillo, that these intruders had been dealt with severely. Jaramillo had assured his old friend that we would act only under his direction, and would not antagonize anyone.

In spite of this, I still felt like a sneak thief, crouching here beside this mountain trail in the darkness. The *pitero,* blowing on the flute, came into view around a bend in the rocky path, walking slowly. The pale moonlight revealed several figures following in single file behind the *pitero.* Two men with lanterns lighted the steps of those following. Three men, with heads bent, were lashing themselves across their backs with short whips almost in cadence to slow, deliberate steps. I gritted my teeth at the sound of the whips striking naked flesh. Four more men followed in the slow procession. They were not using whips, but just what they were doing, I could not make out. All of the men appeared to be fairly young and athletic-looking. With their heads bowed, I could not see their faces. Except for the shrill wailing of the *pito* in the hands of the foremost brother and the shuffling steps on the rocky path, there was no sound. There was no chanting or singing. Only the steady swish and the soggy smack of the whips. They assumed they were alone with their pain and their God and each other. No one saw two pairs of prying eyes. None of them looked our way as they passed within a few feet of our hiding place.

Long after they passed out of our sight down the trail toward the village, we could hear the strange whistling of the flute.

"Damn!" Kerlin muttered, wiping his forehead. He appeared to be sweating, even in the cold of this early April night at seven-thousand-feet altitude. "Did you see that? Who would've believed it?"

"Yeah. And we didn't really get a good look at them."

"Barbaric. Like something out of the Middle

Ages." He seemed shaken. "Even after all we heard about them, I just couldn't believe that civilized people would do such a thing."

"What about those hundreds of men killed at Rorke's Drift? At least no one here dies, unless it's accidental."

"That was different. That was war."

"Oh." I let the subject drop. But I had made my point.

We waited until the procession was gone from sound as well as sight before following slowly down the rocky trail, stumbling and sliding in the blackness. At least the pale light of the moon showed us the worst eroded gullies and the largest rocks. I estimated it to be about eleven o'clock when we reached our camp just outside the village. The Hermano Mayor, through Jaramillo, had made the almost obligatory offer to let us stay in his humble adobe house, but we had declined. I didn't want to put the old man in a bad light with his own people. Besides, since neither Kerlin nor I spoke Spanish, and Jaramillo was spending the night away, it would have created an awkward situation for all concerned. Instead, we preferred to camp by the rented buckboard, taking turns sleeping on it and under it. One of our team of horses had been taken, saddled, and ridden off by Jaramillo to his former village, several miles away. Before leaving, he had turned the other horse over to Sebastian for his own use while we were here. By camping alone, we were free to talk and pretty much do as we pleased, instead of having to accommodate ourselves to the schedule and customs of a Spanish-speaking household. But we were also free to freeze. I began to wonder if I would ever be warm again. Spring would be late in coming to this high mountain valley.

"Juan will be back tomorrow?" Kerlin asked, adding some small pieces of dry wood to our cheery camp fire. We had long since eaten a meager supper and were just trying to drive some warmth into our bodies before rolling into our blankets for the night. Only two lights still showed in the village. The few hundred residents had either gone to bed or their windows were shuttered so tightly no light leaked out.

"He said he would. I hope it's early enough to explain the details of what's going on. He told us there will be a daytime procession."

"Several of them, I understand. From the *morada* to the graveyard and back, with Stations of the Cross along the way."

"If that procession we just saw went to the *morada,* I wonder what they're up to now?"

I shrugged. "Who knows? No one gains entrance to the *morada* except the brothers. Like the kiva was to some of the Pueblos."

"Or the holy of holies to the ancient Jews."

The *morada* was a meeting place, a place of worship, and a place of penance. Jaramillo had told us that each village where a group of

Penitentes existed had one. It was invariably of the same style — a single-story stone or adobe building with a flat roof, sometimes with a wooden cross atop it. The building had one door and possibly one or two windows, was approximately forty feet by twenty feet in size, had a packed dirt floor, and except for a bench or two and some pegs on the walls, was barren of furniture. Sometimes it was divided into two rooms, one for worship and penance and the other for resting or sleeping when the brothers spent extended periods of time there. The main room might also contain a tiny altar with a carving of the agonized Christ on a cross or a wooden carving of the Blessed Virgin Mary or one of the many sharp-featured, bearded *santos*.

After a few minutes of silence, Kerlin stretched and yawned. "This place gives me the oddest feeling. I can't believe we are in the New Mexico Territory in 1879. I feel as if I've been magically transported back to medieval Spain. I'm having trouble believing this is real."

"It's real enough, all right. Or I'm having the same dream. We'll find out tomorrow how real it looks in the daylight."

I did not rest well that night. It was my turn to sleep on the ground. The combination of the dry mountain cold, the hard bed, and the strange environment had me up and down several times in the darkness. Finally, as the sky was pearling, I gave up any attempt at further sleep and stirred up our fire. I tried to keep from waking Kerlin who was sleeping soundly in the back of the buckboard. Apparently, his army training had taught him to sleep anywhere.

Today was Holy Thursday, the day when Christians everywhere commemorate the Last Supper of Christ with His apostles before He was betrayed to the Romans to be crucified. But this was no ordinary Christian village. The men here took up their cross in a literal sense. The followers of Christ believed in suffering with Him.

The day was dawning clear. While the valley lay still in deep, frosty shadow, the sun, behind the bulky mountains, was touching some high, thin clouds with a soft pink. The hush was broken only by some small birds chirping in the chaparral. My breath rose like smoke as I filled the coffeepot from the nearby mountain stream. The fire felt good on my face and hands as I sliced some bacon off the slab and set the blackened frying pan over the fire.

I glanced down at the quiet village of San Jose. If anyone there was stirring, it was not evident. The poor adobe houses were shuttered and silent along the dusty street. From where I crouched at the fire I could see the squat, brooding *morada* a half mile away near the base of a steep slope beyond the village. Were any of the brothers asleep inside, exhausted from a night of bloody self-torture? My imagination conjured up all kinds of morbid images that were probably totally false. I shook my head and turned my attention to the frying bacon.

Just as I set the coffeepot off the fire, Kerlin rolled out of his blanket and sat up.

"Good timing. Breakfast is ready," I greeted him. He grinned and stretched mightily.

"Right you are. I could eat a bear."

"Fried pig will have to do. And mighty little of that. Wish we had a few beans."

"Or potatoes. I have a craving for potatoes that may never be satisfied." He slid off the tail-gate and rubbed the sleep from his eyes. "What's the plan for today?"

"We stay put and see what develops," I said, handing him a steaming tin cup.

"Patience is a virtue I have had to develop in Her Majesty's service."

"I doubt if we'll have too long to wait."

But wait we did. I was keyed up and ready to see all the horrible sights we had been told about, like a patron at some gruesome morality play. But the play was not about to start right away. I didn't really know what I was expecting, but the sun rose as we finished our meager breakfast, had a second cup of coffee, cleaned up our camp, and wandered down close to the village, where we sat in the warming sun on a slope just above the town.

The minutes dragged into hours. The townspeople began appearing on the village street after eight o'clock, but there was not the activity of a normal day. The adults lounged around the upper end of the single street, leaning against adobe walls and smoking cigarettes wrapped in brown paper or cornhusks. Young women nursed babies and lounged with the men. There was only a little desultory conversation among them. What in a more civilized eastern town would have been called a Sabbath hush hung over this New Mexican village. It was an expectant hush, one that we could feel, even from where we sat.

"There's the Hermano Mayor," Kerlin said, pointing. "Let's go down and speak to him."

I demurred. "He doesn't speak English, and we don't speak Spanish." Actually, I was a little nervous about going down among the villagers without the moral support of our mentor, Juan Jaramillo, who had not yet returned from his native village. We had received a few unfriendly glances the day before when we had first arrived. Even though there were visitors from other villages, Kerlin and I were the only Anglos I had seen. But surely, this was to be a Christian religious ceremony. Even though we probably weren't welcome, these people would make no overt move against us. Or so I reasoned.

Finally, about 2:00 p.m., there was a stir in the waiting crowd, and a few minutes later a *pitero* came over the ridge, playing his reed flute, followed by a half dozen women singing a hymn to its doleful accompaniment. Behind them came seven Penitentes, naked to the waist and clad only in white cotton pants cut off at the knees, swinging their short whips, first over one shoulder and then the other in time to their slow, deliberate steps. But this time, unlike last night, their heads, and their identities, were shrouded in black hoods — actually black cotton sacks with holes cut for eyes and mouth.

Kerlin and I had automatically drawn closer and closer to the village street where the procession was passing. No one looked at us or made any move in our direction. The crowd pressed close to the edge of the street as the sorrowful procession went by. Many of the spectators went down on their knees in the dust.

The piper, the women, and the Brothers of Blood, as Jaramillo had called them, passed on to the *campo santo* — the burying ground at the upper end of the town and out of our sight around the last building. Was one of those hooded men Diego Chavez? I had tried to identify him by his size and build. Maybe if I could get a good enough look, I could see the recently healed shoulder wound.

Kerlin and I, by saying nothing, even to each other, and keeping our hats pulled well down over our faces, had managed to make ourselves inconspicuous in the crowd along the village street. It wasn't as if the others didn't know we were there; we were just being tolerated.

A half hour later another piper appeared over

the hill at the lower end of the village from the direction of the *morada.* From a distance of at least two hundred yards, we could hear the *swish, thud, swish, thud* of the cactus whips striking bare flesh, the sound punctuating the strange reed music and the singing of the women. Seven Penitentes were in this procession, four of them whipping themselves and three staggering along under wooden crosses of great size and obvious weight. They gradually approached and passed the spot where we stood and then solemnly wound on down the slope to the graveyard and passed through its low stone wall. They knelt in prayer at several of the graves, kissed the foot of the large wooden cross that stood just inside the arched gateway, and filed out again, returning slowly to the *morada.*

The procession repeated this pilgrimage to the graveyard about forty minutes later, this time with double the number of Penitentes, all hooded and wearing only the short white cotton trousers. Again I watched carefully but could not pick out our friend, Diego Chavez. Just as the procession was leaving the burial ground and returning through the village, one of the men carrying a wooden cross stumbled and fell. Immediately, like a Roman soldier of old, one of the Hermanos de Luz lifted the man to his feet and set the heavy wooden cross over his shoulder once more. When he began to stagger, they helped him along with some kicks to keep him on the path.

Blood was flowing in rivulets and staining the coarse cotton shorts red to the knees of the flagellants. Even though we couldn't see their faces, they gave no sign of pain. They did not flinch, and there was no hesitation in the rigor with which they applied the whips. This was no sham, I noted with amazement, as they passed within a few feet of us.

"Damned masochists!" Kerlin hissed under his breath to me. "Barbarians!"

One more time the doleful procession marched solemnly from the *morada* to the *campo santo* and back, this last time with even more participants than before.

No priests were in evidence. Apparently this shortage of clergy was one of the main reasons the Penitentes had spread and their practices gotten somewhat out of hand.

Then the brothers retired to the *morada,* and we saw no more of them until seven o'clock that evening. Then, in the early darkness of the April night, they came marching down again to the house of José Sebastian, the Hermano Mayor, the largest and finest house in the village. A small family chapel stood a few yards from the house, and the procession turned in that direction. Only two of the hooded brothers were applying the whips to their own backs. Both young men were of a beautiful muscular development and did not appear as scored and lacerated as the men we had seen earlier.

"Probably two new ones," I whispered to Kerlin as the pair dropped to their knees and reverently kissed the foot of a large wooden cross leaning against a tree just outside the chapel. Then they proceeded to walk awkwardly on their knees into the dirt-floored chapel whose back doors stood wide open to accommodate the thirty or forty women who crowded in after the men and knelt down, filling the small room. Kerlin and I squeezed in along the wall with about a dozen men and older children. The hooded flagellants prostrated themselves before the tiny altar. By the wavering candlelight I could see a plaster statue of the Blessed Virgin Mary decked with paper flowers.

But what riveted my attention to the altar was a good-sized crucifix. The carved wooden figure was not a prettified image of Christ I had become accustomed to seeing. This brightly painted figure was the agonized Christ as I had never before seen him depicted — matted hair in the face, blood streaming from the crown of thorns, spike heads protruding from convulsing wrists, skinned knees, stripes of the lash wrapping around the rib cage, body sagging into asphyxiation. But it was the look in the eyes — those windows of the soul — that some talented artist had painted that arrested my gaze. He had created a look that seemed to be saying "Why are you doing this to Me?" as they stared back from the pain of the dying face. This, I reflected with a slight shudder, must have been what it was really like — with all its dirt and blood and screaming nerve ends — an execution in ancient Palestine frozen in time by some obscure New Mexican woodcarver who had evidently worked with his faith as well as his hands. Far from being revulsed by this representation, many of these men were moved to imitate the sufferings they saw before them.

While these thoughts had been going through my mind, the Hermano Mayor raised his cracked voice in leading a hymn. I recognized only a word here and there of the Spanish in the strangely melodious hymn that the crowd around us was singing with obvious deep feeling. After several verses, Sebastian started another hymn, and the singing went on for more than a half hour, the reed flute accompanying.

Then it was over, and the Penitentes retired to Sebastian's house for supper. The Hermanos de Luz, the Brothers of Light, had shuttered the windows and even plugged the keyholes after the Brothers of Blood filed inside.

The crowd outside dispersed, and we headed back toward our wagon.

"Why all the precaution about their identities?" Kerlin asked as we turned aside from the darkened village street. "Certainly these people know who these men are, hoods or not." He shook his head.

"I'd say it was a form of humility. It's like the Pharisees doing good works where everyone could see them. They have their reward by the admiring opinions of the people instead of a reward in heaven."

Kerlin snorted. "I hate to be cynical, but I'm rather convinced it's so they won't be recognized by someone in the crowd and reported to the Church authorities. This is, after all, an underground organization."

"It seems to have the support of everyone we've seen here."

"Curiosity seekers, the most of them," he replied. "If they really supported them, why weren't the majority of them out there abusing themselves along with the few we saw?"

"It's a secret brotherhood that requires an initiation and a certain code of conduct."

"I still say that most of these spectators from other villages were here just to observe the spectacle — not for any religious purpose."

"Maybe." I shrugged, then chose to change the subject. "I wonder when Jaramillo is coming back?"

The next morning, Good Friday, we were in the village bright and early, as was nearly everyone else from the day before. If anything, the crowd was even larger. Having been forewarned by Jaramillo on the trip down that we might very well see an actual crucifixion, we trailed out along the dusty road from the village, along with a few others, toward the *morada*. We took up a position on a slight rise about a hundred yards from the low building and waited.

But it was nearly eleven o'clock when the procession hove in sight from the direction of the village. The *pitero* was leading the way, fingering the now-familiar wailing notes from the reed flute. Then came three brothers, whipping themselves, followed by two dragging large crosses on their shoulders, with about six Hermanos de Luz attending them. Then came Sebastian, reading prayers aloud in Spanish. He was followed by at least half a hundred women and children who dropped to their knees every hundred feet or so to pray, chanting what sounded like some sort of litany of the saints. They bore a plaster statue of the Virgin Mary and a large crucifix with, of all things, a figure of Christ fully clothed in a linen robe.

Reaching the *morada* in their slow march, the Penitentes laid down their crosses and went inside. The women and children knelt on the ground outside and continued their praying and singing of hymns. The Brothers of Light walked around, looking very officious as they waited for their brothers to emerge from the *morada*. Shortly after, they came out again, took up their crosses and whips and started back to town, a short distance away, where they dispersed for some lunch, the Brothers of Blood keeping their black hoods in place as long as they were in sight.

About two o'clock the procession was begun

again, this time with three cross bearers and three using the whips. Kerlin and I had eaten only once in the last twenty-four hours, but food was the last thing on my mind as we watched in fascination at what was passing before us on the way to the *morada.* As they paused to kneel for a few moments on the dusty road just where we stood, I had a chance to look closely at the whips that the Penitentes were using. They were about three and a half feet long, made of yucca cactus fibers, with braided handles. The handles branched out into three tails that smacked loudly on the sufferers' backs as they knelt, hooded heads bowed near us. Every few minutes, the Hermanos de Luz dipped the lashes of these whips into a tin pail of something that I guessed was either some kind of disinfectant or something to make the wounds sting even more. Jaramillo had told us that another crueler whip existed for use as a discipline for any brother who had committed some grievous offense. This whip contained tiny, curved metal tips at the ends of the tails to gouge the flesh with every blow.

But this was real enough and cruel enough. The procession went on its slow way, and we saw three more brothers who, instead of lashing themselves or carrying the heavy crosses, were wearing bundles of buckhorn cactus tied so tightly to their naked backs that the ropes were nearly cutting off circulation in their arms and chests. I cringed at the pain they must have been experiencing as thousands of slender, pointed needles penetrated their backs. But they gave no sign that they even felt it. Yet blood flowed freely, reddening the white canvas trousers.

Were they chewing some sort of pain-killing drug? Was all this for show? There was no indication of it. Their faces were hooded and gave no clue. As the procession slowly filed by, one of the Brothers of Light cut a branch of the *entraña,* or buckhorn, from a roadside bush and threw it on a Penitente who was passing. The needles caught the flesh of his bare shoulder, and the branch hung there! Yet the man gave no sign that he even felt it.

Kerlin and I fell in behind the procession as it made its way through the main street of the village and out the other side, bound for a rocky rise above the graveyard, the road to this New Mexican Calvary.

The group stopped at a prearranged place, and Kerlin and I slid along to where the crowd was thin enough for us to watch the proceedings. Kerlin had said little, but I could sense his disgust at the blood that was flowing from the hooded members of the brotherhood.

A hole, approximately three feet deep, had been dug in the hard earth. The largest of the wooden crosses was laid with its foot near the hole. The man selected to represent Christ stood bravely, arms folded across his chest, black hood hiding his identity, waiting. Two Brothers of Light grabbed him roughly and stretched him out, lashing his arms with ropes to the cross beam. His legs were also tied. Then a large sheet was wound around his entire body, leaving only his arms and feet exposed. Kerlin and I quietly speculated about the reason for this as ropes were tied to the cross beams and the heavy cross was slid to the hole and pulled gradually upright, the heavy foot falling into the post hole with a *thunk.*

"It may be to keep anyone from recognizing him from his scars," I said under my breath.

"They're tying him instead of nailing him," Kerlin observed.

"Well, Jaramillo said they'd had a few deaths in recent years by using spikes instead of ropes. They're not out to kill this man intentionally."

While two Brothers of Light steadied the cross and its human burden by means of a guy rope from each end of the cross beam, the others filled in the hole with rocks and dirt with shovels and hands.

A large rock was placed above five feet from the foot of the cross and another Penitente was led out, wearing only the white cotton pants and the black hood. He had a large bundle of the buckhorn cactus lashed to his naked back. He lay down on his back with his feet toward the cross and used the rock for a pillow. The thick bundle of cactus kept him elevated more than a foot off the ground. It made my flesh cringe to see the cruel thorns penetrating his skin and the hundreds of trickles of blood from as many puncture wounds.

"They must be in some kind of hypnotic state or eating some pain-killing drug," Kerlin growled quietly. "No humans could stand that kind of torture without even flinching."

"I've heard of Indian fakirs who can walk barefoot over live coals," I answered. "Maybe it's all in controlling the mind and the will."

While the substitute Christ was stretched on the cross, the crowd grew gradually silent. I didn't know how long the man could stand this punishment. And I could see nothing of his body except his hands and feet.

We stood near the front of the crowd, less than fifty feet from the cross. A deathly hush had fallen on the place. The only sounds were the breeze rustling in the *piñons* on the hillside nearby. Across the small stream that split the canyon, a prairie dog sat up and barked at the proceedings. The afternoon sun flooded the whole scene — an ancient scene reenacted in this mountain village nineteen centuries later.

Suddenly I was aware of murmuring sounds on the edge of the crowd of spectators, then some angry voices, speaking Spanish. There was a knot of men surrounding someone or something a few yards away.

"Dammit! Lemme alone. I'm not bothering anyone!" a voice yelled angrily in English. "Get your hands off that camera!"

The voice sounded vaguely familiar, and Kerlin and I edged toward the scuffle. The reverent hush was broken as two or three of the villagers grappled with someone. The man's hat was knocked off and I caught a glimpse of a shock of red hair in the sunlight.

"Stay out of it!" Kerlin hissed behind me. "We're the outsiders here."

But I knew that voice, and I knew that hair. When I waded into the group of men, shoving them aside, I saw the face. It was my old friend, Paddy Burke, the photographer! I hadn't seen him since we had parted company a year ago at Fort Bowie in the Arizona Territory.

"Get away from him!" I yelled, slamming a fist into the side of the jaw of a Mexican who had Burke by his collar, pounding him with a fist.

I was suddenly grabbed from both sides and my arms pinned. I could hear Kerlin getting in a few punches behind me as I was slammed to the ground. The breath went out of me. My head spun with the impact.

The crowd was pushing and shoving, and I was being stepped on. Men were tripping over us.

It was all over in only a few seconds. By sheer weight of numbers the men of the village had the three of us pinned. I was dragged to my feet. The faces I saw around me were hostile. No longer were the villagers merely curious, impassive, or mildly disapproving of our presence.

"By God, Matt, what are you doing here?" Paddy Burke said, his face beet-red from his struggles.

"I was just about to ask you the same thing," I replied as the three of us were pushed and hustled away from the crucifixion scene. As I looked back over my shoulder, the horrified looks on the faces of the remaining men and women told me we had committed what amounted to a sacrilege by our violence at this enactment of the Good Friday scene.

As I was jerked roughly toward the village, I caught a glimpse of one burly man picking up a good-sized rock and smashing it down on the wooden camera that lay with its tripod on the ground. The camera was splintered beyond repair.

We were being propelled quickly along the dusty road, surrounded by a sea of angry villagers. I wondered if our fate would be the same as that of the camera.

Even though I had earlier vowed never to go anywhere without my Colt again, I had left my gun belt with my bedroll at the buckboard. None of the villagers I had seen carried a gun, and I didn't want them to think my going armed among them was a sign of aggression. After all, what could happen at Holy Week religious ceremonies? What a fool! Would I never learn to be prepared for anything? My only consolation was that none of my captors seemed to be armed with anything more deadly than homemade clubs and rocks. But these could kill as quickly as a gun. I couldn't really believe that men who were so fervently religious would actually murder us. But how could I be sure? Those who were capable of doing so much violence to their own bodies would surely think nothing of doing violence to meddling strangers. There were probably a few knives concealed under their loose clothing.

"I told you we should have kept to ourselves," Kerlin said quietly in his thick brogue as the three of us were herded into an empty adobe hut on the edge of the village and thrown roughly on the dirt floor. We crawled a few feet and sat up with our backs against the wall. The dark faces that crowded around us were excited, as the villagers spoke and gestured to each other rapidly. I could catch only an occasional word here and there. My Spanish was minimal, and this was much too rapid for me to get even the drift of the conversation or arguments. I could only guess, from the heat of the discussion, that they were not in total agreement as to what to do with us.

It was typical of the fiery Paddy Burke that his face showed more anger than fear. The first time I had seen him, he had been surrounded and under attack by Apaches, but he was still taking the fight to them. How could I think that he would be afraid in this situation?

"Never thought I'd see you in a place like this," I said quietly to Burke, next to me, as our captors continued to talk to each other. They were making no attempt to tie us. Maybe they were going to do away with us quickly. In any case, we were not going anywhere while this crowd hemmed us in.

"Hell, think what a great picture this would make — a modern-day crucifixion. Think how many views of that I could sell!"

I shook my head. "Fools rush in . . ." I said. "You haven't changed a bit. Now your camera's busted, and we might be before this is over."

He looked over at me and seemed to soften a little. "Thanks for coming to help, even though it didn't do a lot of good. I appreciate it."

I gave him a half smile. "Did your picture of that lynching last year make your reputation?"

"I sold a lot of those stereoscopic views. I don't know how famous it made me, but I *am* pretty well known now. And that view got me out of a really tight money situation. I've got a new team and wagon and a couple of new cameras. And I was able to send my mother enough in New York so she could stop working and live in a decent house."

"Well, you should have known better than to come into this village with that camera. We had an introduction from a native, and we still got some hard looks."

He shrugged. "I bribed the wrong man. He disappeared with my money without getting me permission from the Hermano Mayor to take some views of this. You have to take some chances in this business. It would have been a great shot if I could have gotten it. Maybe next time . . ."

"You're crazy."

"I wish I could understand Spanish," Kerlin said, leaning forward around Burke. "What do you think these fanatics have planned for us?" His voice showed no fear, but he was cautious. I could see from the tension in his muscular body that the Irishman was ready to go down fighting, if necessary.

After a vociferous discussion, which we did not understand, several of the villagers went outside, leaving us in the custody of about fifteen men. Apparently, our fate, whatever it was to be, had been decided. Our hard-eyed captors were armed with clubs and rocks, and two of them had three-foot cactus-fiber whips, apparently borrowed from the *morada.*

But we waited. Nothing happened immediately. The minutes dragged. It began to get hot and stuffy in the airless room. The dark New Mexicans were all wearing coarse cotton pants and shirts, sandals or heavy work shoes; some wore felt hats. To a man their faces were grim. When they looked at us, it required no translation to know the hate that was focused on the meddling gringos.

I slipped out my watch and glanced at it. A good half hour had dragged by. Two of my captors looked greedily at the gold-plated watch. From the looks of their garb and their village, I knew they must live a hand-to-mouth existence. In our present circumstances, any one of these hard-eyed men could have taken the watch from me, with no one the wiser. But no one made a move to touch me. These men, I suddenly realized, were not Mexican bandits. They were only dirt-poor descendants of the Spanish conquerors, living in a remote mountain village and trying to practice their religion in peace. That it was allegedly the same religion I professed was still a mystery to me.

The man who had eyed my Waltham timepiece with most interest turned away and rolled himself a brown-paper cigarette. He lit it, inhaled, and blew smoke out of both nostrils. The temptation to relieve me of the watch must have been great. He avoided looking at me. I wondered what was going on in his mind. Was he really disinterested? Was he held back because of the commandment, "Thou Shalt Not Steal," or was he afraid his fellows would see him take it?

It suddenly dawned on me that we were probably being held out of sight and sound until the poor Penitente who was bound to the cross a few hundred yards from where we sat was finally cut down and carried off to be revived — or to die.

Burke wiped his perspiring face on his shirtsleeve, while Kerlin's head had dropped forward on his knees, and he appeared to doze in the close atmosphere. A scorpion crept out of a large crack between the adobe bricks near me, paused, tail curled over its back, and then scurried away along the base of the wall.

If I had only kept my gun with me, I could have backed this crowd away, and we could have made a break for our buckboard. But then I remembered that Jaramillo had one of our horses and the Hermano Mayor had penned up the other somewhere in the village. But how had Burke gotten here? Where had he left his wagon or his horse and pack animal?

I was on the verge of asking him when a man stepped in the open doorway. *"Vamanos!"* he said.

Several men immediately grabbed the three of us and jerked us to our feet. We were crowded out the door into the street. I blinked and squinted in the sudden brightness of the afternoon sun.

Someone propelled me forward with a kick from behind. I stumbled and fell, the anger rising in me. I jumped to my feet and turned to face my tormentors as Kerlin and Burke were both shoved past me. I realized we were being put on the rocky road that wound north out of town through the mountains. I swallowed my anger. If we were merely being run out of town, we were getting off lucky. Better to go peaceably for now. We could always sneak back later, under cover of darkness, and recover our rig, if it was still there, or get to Burke's rolling darkroom, if it was parked somewhere in the area.

But it was not to be that easy. As I turned my back to follow my companions, I heard an expletive in Spanish close behind me. An instant later a cactus lash burned across my back. I gasped at the sudden, searing pain of it.

"Damn your hide!" Burke yelled.

From my hands and knees I dimly saw him leap at a man of medium size who was drawing back the whip for another stroke. Three more men with whips lashed out at him as Kerlin jumped into the melee, fists swinging. I staggered to my feet as fast as I could and dove at the nearest man, who brought the whip savagely across my body. The whip landed, but so did I, tackling him as my shoulder drove into his legs. I remember being surprised at how easily he went down. Then everything blurred into a world of choking dust and stinging pain and curses, as bodies thumped and crashed around me. I could hear the whistling of whips and a sandaled foot caught me in the side of the jaw.

Then it was over. I didn't know what happened until I felt callused hands dragging me back and was suddenly aware that the fighting had stopped. I ran a hand across the sweat and grime on my face as I sat stupidly on the ground. When my fingers came away red I realized for the first time I wasn't sweating. It was blood.

Juan Jaramillo and José Sebastian stood there, separating us. The old, withered Sebastian spoke, his words crackling like a fire of *piñon* logs, as he looked from one to another of us and then at the villagers. I had no idea whether he was berating us or them, or both. I was almost glad I couldn't understand him.

"This is shameful, disgraceful!" Jaramillo said in English when the older man paused for breath. His dark face looked like a thundercloud. "I leave you alone on your honor for a few days, and I come back to find this!" He turned and spoke in Spanish to Sebastian, and

I gathered from the tone of his voice that he was apologizing.

I got to my feet, and the shirt I was wearing almost fell off. The whips had cut the back out of it, and it was held together only by the collar.

"Who is this man?" Jaramillo snapped, indicating the redheaded Burke.

"Paddy Burke, a photographer friend of mine," I replied quickly before Burke could say anything. "He was attacked by the villagers when he tried to record the crucifixion. We came to his aid. That's all there is to it."

"That's all? Didn't I warn you about antagonizing these people? Surely you knew better than to try to capture a photograph of these ceremonies."

"He didn't know," I said, again cutting off Burke as he tried to speak. "He thought he had permission, but the man who gave it was not from this village." This was not completely truthful, but I had to smooth this thing over as best I could. Jaramillo was our only mediator.

Jaramillo spoke again to the Hermano Mayor in Spanish, gesturing and pointing. The old man replied and then said something to the dozen or so men who were nursing a few bruises and cuts of their own. They began muttering softly to each other and then turned and began to disperse. My explanation, unconvincing as it sounded, had apparently done the trick. I was glad Burke had taken my cue and curbed his tongue and his temper.

"Come. We are leaving this village — now." Jaramillo strode away without another word.

Kerlin, Burke, and I found ourselves standing alone in the middle of the road, with only small groups of women and children eyeing us curiously from a safe distance.

I could feel blood trickling down my face and torso from several small wounds. Even though I felt sore from the pounding and the open cuts were stinging, I was all right. Kerlin's left eye was swollen and discoloring, while Burke had slashes across his face, neck, and forearm and was feeling gingerly of a lump on his head.

"Well, I didn't lose any teeth in that fracas, anyway." He grinned.

"Those men aren't big, but they sure are strong," I observed as we walked away from the road to circle the village and get to our buckboard parked near the creek.

Jaramillo was leading his horse away, walking with Sebastian. It was just as well. I didn't want to talk to the older man until he cooled off. I had a feeling it was going to be a long, uncomfortable ride back to Colorado.

We bathed our wounds in the cold, clear water of the stream near our camp. I removed the remains of my torn, bloody shirt. The warm afternoon sun felt good on my back even as I shivered at the touch of the icy water. I squatted and scooped some of the water into my mouth, wincing slightly as the cold hurt my teeth. But it helped numb the cuts inside my cheek where the kick had caught me on the jaw.

"Sorry to get you boys into this mess," Burke said, standing up and wiping the water from his face.

"We dealt ourselves in," I answered, spitting out the water.

Kerlin said nothing.

"I can replace that camera. It was pretty old and scarred up anyway."

"You don't work with an apprentice or an assistant anymore?" I asked.

"Not since Chris went back home a few months back. I'd like to get one, but not just anybody. It has to be somebody who really wants to learn and isn't lazy. When you spend most of your time in the field, you'd better be working with somebody you can get along with."

I nodded. "Where's your wagon?"

"Left it about a mile south of here, down in a draw. Walked up here early this morning with all that gear on my back — camera, dark tent, tripod, and chemicals." He chuckled. "That's one reason I need a new assistant — a strong one."

Burke was a small-to-average-sized man but was stringy-tough. No one was going to get the best of this red-haired New Yorker. I had found that out last year when I had seen him in action in the Arizona Territory. And getting a great photograph was his all-consuming artistic obsession. It was the driving force that made him brave all kinds of danger and discomfort.

"Where're you off to from here?" I inquired, pulling my jacket out of my bedroll and slipping it on over my bare skin. The ridged welts on my back were no longer bleeding. I was glad I couldn't see them.

"Down south into the desert until the weather warms up some."

He extended his hand to me. "Good to see you again, Matt. I'd better be on my way before those Mexicans decide they haven't had enough." He grinned. "I want to see if I can retrieve that tripod on my way out if it isn't broken."

"We're going back north. To the Denver and Rio Grande Railroad." I briefly explained to him what had transpired since I had last seen him.

"Sounds like you've had enough excitement for two or three men. My life sounds godawful dull by comparison."

I shook hands with Burke, and he offered his hand to Kerlin who, after a hesitation, took it with a short nod.

Burke waved and walked off toward the village, just as Jaramillo appeared, leading the horse he had lent Sebastian. He was also leading the horse he had ridden. We got ready to hitch up for the ride home.

The ride back to Pueblo was, for the most part, a silent trip. We took turns driving the buckboard. The road was rough and nothing more than a rocky trail in most places, and the unsprung wagon made for a jolting ride.

We camped as soon as it got full dark that night. Even though Jaramillo generally knew the way, it had been many years since he had been over this road, and even he couldn't keep to it in the dark. We didn't linger over our cooking fire but hit our blankets early. We were all tired and sore and out of sorts. Kerlin had grown unusually quiet. I didn't know if it was because of what he had seen or because of being irritated with me for drawing him into a fight he wanted no part of. Jaramillo, I felt sure, was angry that he had let these two gringos talk him into bringing them to the village to witness a secret ceremony. And these white outsiders had betrayed his confidence by creating a wild disturbance. I was sure the older man felt keenly the loss of face with his former friends. I wondered whether I should attempt to explain our side of what had happened. But I decided against it for the time. Wrapped, fully clothed, in my blanket, I tried to ease my tired, sore body into something that resembled a comfortable position.

The next day was Holy Saturday. Spring was trying its best to burst forth in the southern Rockies, perhaps in preparation for Easter Sunday. The sun knocked the chill off, and by noon the windless air was positively warm. Mountain wildflowers were stretching their faces toward the sun on the southern flanks of the dun-colored hills. Even though there were still pockets of snow in the sheltered areas, and the air was cold in the shade, there was a definite smell of spring in the air.

We jolted along the ever-ascending road that wound among the hills. Sundown found us finally approaching the long summit of Raton Pass on the toll road run for several years by Uncle Dick Wooten, an early frontiersman who kept a hotel at the top of the pass on the stage road. By this time the horses were pretty well used up, and so were we. Even though we had not pushed hard, we had started early and come a long way, mostly uphill. It didn't take much for us to decide to spend the night under a roof at Wooten's place.

By this time I felt better about our trip because I had selected an opportunity during the day to breach the cold silence and explain to

Jaramillo exactly what had occurred at the village. He seemed to accept my story, which obviously differed from the one Sebastian had told him.

By the time we drew rein in front of the low, log stage stop with the smoke issuing from the chimney, I think I had him convinced that we had not betrayed his confidence in us. He didn't say much, but I attributed this more to fatigue than to irritation with the way our trip had turned out. Over a mug of hot rum in front of a crackling fire in the tavern room that evening, Jaramillo unbent somewhat. He told us he had ridden over to his old village and discovered a lady who had been his sweetheart nearly twenty years before.

"Ah, it was a joy to go back and see many of those I knew long ago. But many of my old friends are dead and gone. And the young ones are nearly grown. So many new faces." He shook his head sadly. "But even in the midst of remembering, I see Angela — nearly as beautiful as when I left many years ago."

The flames from the log fire seemed to etch the lines deeper in his strong, hawklike face. "It was as if I had never been away. Her husband is dead — killed in a mine cave-in. She wanted me and I wanted her. The fire was still there between us." He took a deep draught of his rum from the pewter mug. "What irony!" He snorted a short laugh. "Beset by temptation in the midst of trying to expiate my past sins!"

I could see the corded jaw muscles working as he ground his teeth in frustration. "It was a temptation of the flesh that only the lash could subdue." He looked up at me across the table. "I hope now your eyes are opened to see what Los Hermanos Penitentes are about." He set his mug down and rose stiffly to his feet. "I believe that I will take to my bed. It has been a long and trying day."

With that, he nodded to us and moved stiffly away.

It was only then that I realized he had gone back, not only to renew old acquaintances, but had also somehow persuaded the Hermano Mayor of his village to let him take an active part in the self-flagellation with the brothers of his old *morada*. If I could get a look at his back, I could confirm my suspicions. He was right. My eyes *had* been opened, and I felt almost a kinship with the Penitentes. The fight that had ensued with the villagers was already fading from my memory. I did not hold them at fault; I probably would have done the same thing in their position. But, as I glanced over at Kerlin who was staring moodily into his mug, I sensed that he did not feel the same about it. And yet he had been the one who had been so eager to follow Chavez and observe the Penitente rites. My Irish friend had been very moody since he had actually seen the severe penances being practiced. The fight had not improved his disposition.

"Too bad we're not near enough to a town or a mission to attend Mass in the morning. Easter Sunday," I remarked.

"Aye. 'Tis a shame, all right."

"Even if we had stayed in the village, there was no priest."

He nodded absently. "A barbaric practice, that," he remarked, almost to himself. "I can't understand why the Church doesn't excommunicate the lot of them."

I started to reply but then thought better of it. Kerlin, for some reason I couldn't fathom, could not accept the fact that this medieval penance was still being practiced by devout Catholics. If these people had belonged to some African tribe, I felt Kerlin could have accepted it with no trouble. But this way it hit too close to home. And it disturbed him to know that the members of his own religion were capable of such things. I hoped he wouldn't take out his feelings on Diego Chavez.

The next day we drove down off the mountain pass and along the stage road to Trinidad. We didn't arrive back in Pueblo until late morning on Monday. We turned in the rig to the livery, and Jaramillo, after a brief good-bye, went to a hotel to await the next train north to Denver.

I felt somewhat disoriented coming back to the mundane life of a railroad laborer after what we had witnessed and experienced the past week. It was as if I had been on the moon and was just returning to earth. How could everyone act just the same after what had been going on in the New Mexican villages south of us? Wasn't the world somehow different? But nothing had outwardly changed here, I noted, as Kerlin and I walked out to the boxcar camp at the edge of town Monday afternoon.

The temporary D&RG laborers' camp appeared nearly deserted. Crenshaw was nowhere to be seen. Apparently, most of the men were also gone somewhere on a work detail.

"I knew we should have rested up in town overnight and then come back out here in the morning," Kerlin grumbled as we looked around the dreary, muddy camp that was gradually drying out in the warm sun. The snow had melted, but the ground must have still been frozen a few inches down since none of the puddles had soaked in.

"Let's check the mess car," I suggested.

One of the cooks was lounging, in shirtsleeves and apron, on the sunny side of the car. He puffed on a short pipe as he sat on the steps, elbows on knees.

"Crenshaw around anyplace?" I asked.

He took the pipe from his mouth and cocked an eyebrow at us, squinting up into the sun.

"Where you two been?"

"Away for a week or so," I replied shortly. "Where's Crenshaw?"

"You ain't heard about it?"

"About what?" I was becoming a little irritated.

"All the excitement. Hell, the Santa Fe has called in some big guns. A whole carload o' hard cases from Dodge City rolled in last Wednesday. Musta been thirty of them. And ya know who was leading them? Bat Masterson, that's who!"

"Who is Bat Masterson?" Kerlin wanted to know.

"A famous, or infamous, peace officer or gunfighter — take your pick," I answered. "He has quite a reputation as a good man with a gun. He's a leader. Not afraid of the devil himself, I understand."

"What's his stake in this?" I asked the cook.

"Dunno. Reckon the Santa Fe is payin' top dollar for the best artillery they can find. They must be gettin' serious about takin' and keepin' that Royal Gorge."

"Well, the Supreme Court hasn't ruled on it yet. It must be a bluff to scare off General Palmer and the D and RG."

"Wal, all I know is, it sure has been keepin' the boys occupied these past few days. Most o' them been up the Gorge and around Canon City." He chuckled. "At least they ain't been hangin' around camp, gripin' about the food and pesterin' me. I got lotsa time to take it easy for a change."

"Where are Masterson and his gunhands now?" I cut in.

"Dunno for sure. Last I heard, they was up t' Canon City tryin' t' decide if they wanted to tackle our stronghold in the Gorge."

"We're holding the Gorge?"

"Yup. Old Gil Latham, one of our engineers, heard they was comin', so he rounded up a bunch o' the boys, and he and Crenshaw skedaddled up t' Canon City on a fast train and then barricaded themselves in one o' them stone forts in the Gorge. Then they just dared Masterson to come and try t' root 'em out." He spat to one side and then grinned hugely. "Last I heard, Bat was puffin' and blowin', but he was sure stayin' safe in Canon City."

"Mike, I'm going into town and get my horse out of the livery. It's high time he got some exercise. You want to rent a horse and ride up to Canon City with me?"

He shed his morose mood instantly. "Sounds like a fine idea to me," he replied, catching up as I started off at a trot toward town. "But what will we do when we get there?"

"We'll decide on the way. But I didn't sign on this outfit to miss all the excitement. Sounds like we left at the wrong time. Things are coming to a head without us."

But the ride to Canon City proved to be rather futile. We arrived just at dusk, and the town seemed relatively quiet. We drew our horses up at the largest saloon, whose lights were illuminating the street of the small town.

It appeared to be the only place on the main street that looked alive. The door had been propped open to admit some air and let out some of the smoke. The place was about half full. We drew only cursory glances as we edged up to the bar and ordered beer.

"Damned if I wouldn't prefer a good, dark Guinness to this pale swill," Kerlin growled, wiping the foam from his mustache with the back of his hand.

Everyone in the saloon was a stranger to me. Kerlin did not recognize any of the patrons as D&RG men either. Some were playing cards; some were just drinking and talking. A few were eating supper.

The man leaning on the bar next to me was of average height but lean and muscular of build. He wore a hat set well back on his head and had a sweeping brown mustache. I guessed him to be in his late twenties. He spoke to no one, but looked straight ahead at the stacked glasses on the back bar and nursed a tumbler of whiskey.

"What's a man do for excitement in this town?" I asked.

He eyed me from under bushy brows before he straightened up. "Dunno. I'm new here myself."

"This place is doin' a lot better business than when I was through here last," I continued.

"That so?" The tone was totally indifferent.

"All these men must work for that new railroad I hear tell they're buildin' around here."

The man finally looked directly at me. "You must be from a long way off if you ain't heard what's been goin' on around here."

"Yeah. Me and my partner just come up from the Arizona Territory lookin' for work. We been doin' some muckin' in the Silver King Mine, but we got tired o' that. I like to be able to see the blue sky and smell fresh air when I work. Heard they was puttin' on some men around these parts. Reckon a couple o' able-bodied men could get work railroadin'?"

"That depends on who you want to work for," the young man answered carefully. "You two got yourselves smack dab in the middle of a war. You'd be smarter just to keep movin'."

"War? What war?"

"Nothin'. Sorry I mentioned it." He drained his glass and held it up to get the bartender's attention.

"I'd be obliged to ya, mister, to tell us what's goin' on," I urged, still affecting total ignorance.

"Look," he said, sipping at his fresh drink, "the Denver and Rio Grande Railroad is tryin' to build a railroad through the Royal Gorge here. There ain't room but for one road into the mountains. The Atchison, Topeka and Santa Fe is determined to build a road through the same gorge. The Supreme Court is tryin' to decide who gets it. But the Rio Grande people have done jumped the gun and are holed up in the Gorge, just darin' anybody to take 'em out. Course that ain't fair until the Court decides, so the Santa Fe, who's already run a line across Kansas, has hired a few of us to root 'em outa there. That's about it in a nutshell."

"Wal, if that don't put horns on a toad," I marveled in my best stage manner. "How does a man go about joining up? Me and my partner'd like to get in on some o' this action. How much does it pay?"

"I think we got all the help we need," he replied, eyeing me up and down, noting the Colt I wore. "Besides, you don't look like the type who'd care to get shot at for three dollars a day."

"Three dollars! That's pretty low wages, all right. We got five for a ten-hour shift in the mines. Has there been a lot o' lead flyin' already?"

"Not so's you could notice it," he replied, leaning on the bar again and sipping at his jigger.

I turned around and leaned my back against the bar. I wanted to ask if Bat Masterson was in the room but couldn't figure out a way to do it without alerting the man that I was more aware of the situation than I let on.

"Were all these boys just brought in by the Santa Fe?" I finally asked, indicating the room.

"Yeah. Most of them, anyway. We came in from Dodge City. Bat Masterson is leading us."

"Not the famous Marshal Bat Masterson

from Dodge?" I marveled.

"The very one," the man replied, obviously pleased at the awe in my voice.

"Which one is he?"

He turned and scanned the room. "That one right back there." He pointed at a table about thirty feet away. "The one in the black derby smoking a cigar."

I picked him out immediately. He sat facing me, leaning back in his chair, scanning a poker hand. Then he put his cards facedown and leaned forward, removing the cigar and tossing two chips on the pile in front of him. He had a rather round face, thick black eyebrows, and a black mustache. But it was his eyes that were his most arresting feature. They were a startling blue. A handsome man. He looked to be of a stocky build under the black coat and vest. I had heard he was a fancy dresser, and such was the case, even to the diamond stickpin in his cravat.

Most of the other men in the room were dressed in work clothes, plaid shirts, or shirts of gray or blue, with vests. To a man they were well armed. But they were obviously not thinking of business just now, as two or three of them got up to dance with the saloon girls who were waiting tables. The piano player was pounding out "Buffalo Gal."

"All the D and RG lads must be up the canyon, or at another pub, or someplace besides here," Kerlin said quietly to me under cover of the noise in the room.

I nodded. It was about time to leave and find a safe place to spend the night.

I turned back to the bar. "Well, we're gettin' down to our last few dollars. But you're right," I said to the Dodge City gunhand next to me. "I don't hanker to get shot at for three dollars a day. Guess we'll just be movin' on t' see if we can get work. Maybe hook up with some wagoneers over in the San Luis Valley or one of the ranches north of here."

"Tell you what," the man replied, the whiskey apparently loosening his tongue, "the Santa Fe's hiring 'most everybody who wants to join up. It'd give ya a little money to see ya through for a few days."

"What about this shootin'? I don't aim to get involved in no shootin' war if I can help it."

"Don't worry about that. All we've done mostly is sit around since we been here. About the only thing we've killed is time. And that's gettin' harder to do every damn day."

"Well . . ." I appeared to waver at this suggestion of a possible job.

"Matter of fact," he continued, reaching for a bottle on the bar and helping himself to another tumbler of whiskey, "if you can keep a secret, I'll let you in on somethin' about this war."

"Sure." I nodded solemnly.

He looked around, conspiratorially, and then tried to focus his eyes on me again. "All us boys are up here from Dodge just to have a little fun. We ain't figurin' to get shot, and we ain't aimin' to shoot nobody, either."

I gave him a curious look but waited for him to continue.

"Now, if you ever mention this, I'll deny I ever said it."

I nodded, wondering what he was getting at.

"All the Santa Fe boys and the D and RG boys are shootin' *blanks* at each other!"

"No!" I had a terrific urge to burst out laughing, but I managed to choke it back. "Really?" I actually didn't know whether to believe him or not. He could have been playing me for a sucker, just to have a good laugh at my expense. Some practical joke to liven up the boredom, hoping we would go along and make fools of ourselves.

"You're damn right," he continued. "Of course, if the bosses ever find out, we'll all be fired."

"How do you know the D and RG boys are usin' blanks?" I asked cautiously.

"Well, a few of our boys got to mingling with a few of the D and RG at the faro tables and parlor houses down in Pueblo. The upshot o' the whole thing was that the Rio Grande boys said, 'We ain't out to shoot you if you ain't out to shoot us.' Our boys agreed, and that was about the size of it. The rest of us got the word on the sly. Hell, it's got to be kind of fun so far. We make a big show of blastin' hell outa each other, but nobody gets hit. Guess we're just bad shots. His shoulders shook with laughter as he hunched over his drink. "Except for the bigwigs, who gives a damn which railroad builds through that canyon? We're still gettin' our same daily wages. When this is over, I'll be back to clerkin' at the hotel in Dodge and buyin' into the dry goods store as I can afford it. I'm no professional gunfighter." He glanced down at my empty mug. "Buy you another beer?"

"Thanks, but no. We've got to be gettin' on. I may take your advice about hirin' on. Where do we find the foreman in the morning?"

He waved his arm vaguely. "Just ask around tomorrow. Somebody'll tell ya where to find him. He's usually up earlier than the rest of us." The liquor was obviously beginning to have a strong effect on him.

I nudged Kerlin, and we headed for the door.

It was all true. We discovered just how true the next day when we left our horses at the Canon City livery and walked into the canyon the few miles to the site of the first D&RG rock fortress.

When we got within a couple hundred yards of the rock fortification that I recalled so well from our last foray into the Gorge, Kerlin and I yelled and made plenty of noise to identify ourselves as friends. Only then did we proceed cautiously forward and were finally recognized. We were not taking any chances on getting shot by our own men. But the chances of that were slim, we found out. The use of blank cartridges was a common joke among the twenty or thirty men manning this particular barricade. More men were stationed at two or three stone forts strung out upstream for several miles. Even though there was plenty of live ammunition present, as far as I could find out, the only live rounds were in the rifles of the foreman, Crenshaw, and four or five others. Crenshaw, in particular, was furious that nearly all the men the road had recruited were only playing games with the enemy.

"Damnedest thing I ever saw," he said with a snort when I broached the subject. "Grown men playing at war. Likely to get themselves killed. I wonder if they think Bat Masterson will only be bustin' caps when he comes against us? If we lose this gorge to the Santa Fe, we'll all be lookin' for work."

"Don't be gettin' your dander up, Crenshaw," Gil Latham said, strolling over just then and leaning his tall frame on the chest-high stone wall. "If they decide to get serious, then we can, too." He shot a stream of tobacco juice over the barricade and grinned, wiping his mouth with the back of his hand. "This is a publicity war we're fightin' here. None of this is going to mean a damn thing once the Supreme Court gets around to making its ruling. This is a war of strategy, a war of nerves, not a war of bullets. At least not yet."

"Good thing I'm not your boss," Crenshaw replied without smiling. "You'd be out runnin' the trains instead of sitting around up here."

"If it hadn't been for my quick thinking and Carl Remmer's okay, the Santa Fe men would have possession of this canyon right now."

"Who's Remmer?" I asked.

"The civil engineer who's directly in command of this road. He works right under General Palmer, the founder, owner, and financial wizard of the D and RG," Latham replied.

"How *is* the road getting along without you?" I asked. "We don't have that many engineers, do we?"

Latham shrugged. "Enough to keep things running to a degree. Two of the other engineers are filling in for me. Besides, I don't plan to be here that long."

"And just where in hell do you think you're going, and when?" Crenshaw demanded. "Do you think the Santa Fe men are going to let you or any of us just walk out of here without some fireworks or bustin' a few heads? We may have the canyon for now, but we're stuck here while Masterson and his boys keep the rathole plugged by sitting there in Canon City. And you two are stuck with us," he added, looking at me and Kerlin. "I don't buy that line about shootin' blanks. If you think those Dodge City boys are shooting blanks, you're bigger fools than I first took you for."

"The man seems a little loose with his tongue," Kerlin observed to me in his heaviest brogue, plenty loud enough for all of us to hear. "I'm thinkin' we should be hearin' an apology for being called fools." He shot a hard look at the short, stocky foreman.

Their glances locked for a moment. Then Crenshaw dropped his eyes. "Okay. Okay. Forget I said anything. But you'll remember I warned you. It may seem like a picnic now, but wait'll we begin to run outa grub." He glanced around and said, "I don't reckon Chavez came back with you, did he?"

"Nope. Haven't seen him," I replied truthfully. If he had been among the Penitentes we saw, we had not been able to identify him.

"Don't reckon we'll see that little Mex again," he growled. "Just as well. We got more men than we can use now." He yanked his hat brim down and walked away.

"You boys want to join me for a little lunch?" Latham asked after Crenshaw had gone.

"Sure."

He led the way back along the rocky benchland near the river where my old friend, Gregory DeArmand, the stoker, was squatting over a smoky fire, frying some kind of meat and beans in a small skillet.

"Matt, it's good to see you," he boomed, setting the pan down on a rock and embracing me in a huge bear hug. I introduced him to Kerlin, whom he had not met.

Latham set about fixing the coffee while we talked. We answered the big fireman's questions and brought them up to date on what we had seen of the Penitentes.

"It was an experience I'll never forget," I concluded. "And we have you to thank for it. Gil, if you hadn't put us in touch with Juan Jaramillo, we would never have been able to follow Chavez to that village. In fact, I don't know if he was even in San Jose. We were never able to spot him. So, tell us what's been going on here. I was afraid we'd missed all the fun, when we reported back to Pueblo and found everybody gone."

"General Palmer intercepted a telegram at Colorado Springs that the Santa Fe sent to Dodge, calling for help in holding the canyon. The general passed the word to Carl Remmer, who told me to have a train loaded and ready to roll within the hour. That was last Wednesday. And here we've been ever since. About three dozen men are upcanyon a few miles at the next barricade. There are still three crews outside, working the trains and about two dozen maintaining the tracks."

"We saw your train on a siding at Canon City," I said.

"We left four armed men there to guard it. We didn't know what to expect, but we couldn't bring the train any farther. I think we should have laid some track into the Gorge earlier when we had the chance."

"By the time we got to it, the Santa Fe men were here last year," Gil added.

"I expect you left some brave lads with the train," Kerlin said.

"They're a tough crew, all right," DeArmand replied, "but we really don't expect any serious threat to capture that train. The Santa Fe doesn't want to put itself on the wrong side of the law by attacking or taking over any D and RG property by force. They want to pressure us here in the canyon."

"I thought the Santa Fe had control of the D and RG under that lease Palmer was forced to agree to," I said, shoving a piece of fried bread into my mouth. "So they wouldn't actually be attacking anyone else's property."

"Technically, you're right, but the two roads are still run separately, and the public views them that way," Latham replied. "This whole business gets more and more confusing. That's one reason most of us aren't taking this thing too seriously. We aren't about to kill each other over it."

"I wish the Supreme Court would get off their rear ends and make some kind of decision on this," I remarked.

"Two railroads fighting over a mountain pass is probably last on their agenda." DeArmand grinned.

"There are some principles of law involved here that should get their attention," Latham said, sitting cross-legged on the ground with a tin plate in front of him. "Besides, this thing has been in and out of Colorado courts for years, so it's not like it's some new issue that just popped up."

"Have any of the Santa Fe men attacked you here yet?" Kerlin asked.

"Sure. Regularly. At least once every day, a few of them will come up the canyon and we'll pop away at each other for maybe thirty minutes, and then they disappear," DeArmand said. "Nobody gets hurt."

"Do you reckon Bat Masterson is in on this ruse?" I said. "This is the craziest thing I've ever heard of." I shook my head and held out my tin cup for Kerlin to refill it from the black pot. "Has Remmer been in touch with you since you came in here?"

"No. And I'm thinking it's about time for me and DeArmand to get out and go to running our train again. This may settle into a long siege," Gil Latham said.

"Crenshaw seemed to think that the Santa Fe bunch will get serious if any of you tries to leave," I remarked.

"Crenshaw will worry himself into an early grave," Latham said. "He has no imagination. Sees nothing but the dark side of everything."

"That distrust and caution may be what's kept him alive," I observed. "I'll have to say he was the one who got us out of this canyon alive back in February. By the way, did that rock slide block much of the river?"

"Less than a third of it," DeArmand said. "The Santa Fe crew cleared all that rubble from the base of the wall in about two weeks. The canyon is open all the way through again."

I took a deep breath of the fresh air. This place looked so different from when I had last seen it under a blanket of ice and snow, a bitter wind clawing at us as we half carried the wounded Chavez out. Now the place resembled a picnic ground, with groups of men milling around cooking fires, the snow gone, and the warm spring sun beaming down on us. The Arkansas River was full to overflowing with snow melt, and the steady rushing of its waters formed a backdrop to every other sound.

"If you two are ready to leave here, Mike and I are heading back for Canon City tonight. If you were serious about getting out of here, we can all make a break for it together," I offered as I dropped my plate and cup into a nearby bucket of water.

Something buzzed past my ear like a bumblebee before I even heard the sound of the shot. The next instant I was flat on the ground, spilling the bucket of water and dirty dishes all over myself. A volley of shots cracked off somewhere behind me, and the booming echoes bounced back and forth from the rock walls. I scrambled around and yanked my Colt, thinking how close I had come to having my head taken off by one of the "blank" rifle shells.

"Ah, the afternoon party has started," Latham said, reaching for the rifle he had propped against a nearby rock.

"You better get your ass on the ground before it gets shot off!" I yelled at him. "Those are real bullets!"

He dropped to one knee, giving me a quick look as his face went pale.

Chips flew from the boulders of the barricade as other men were shouting and grabbing their weapons, suddenly realizing that we were under a real attack.

The four of us scuttled toward the protection of the five-feet-high rock wall. I marveled at how quickly the big DeArmand could move when he had to.

"I hope you've got some live ammunition for that thing," I said to Latham as we crouched behind the rocks, listening to the shots banging and booming. Kerlin was on one knee next to me, checking the loads in his Adams double-action.

"Looks like Crenshaw was right."

"Those are the most realistic blanks I've ever seen."

The moon was still hidden by the sheer rock walls and the bottom of the canyon was in inky blackness as the four of us dropped softly over the barricade that night a little after ten. Our sentries had been alerted so we wouldn't get ourselves shot before we got out of range of the fortress. The cartridge loops of our gun belts were full. Latham and DeArmand carried Winchester carbines. Kerlin and I had our handguns. Only the Irishman's .450 Adams was not an interchangeable caliber with our weapons' .44-40. But he had brought an adequate supply of shells for his own British revolver.

That noon attack had been the first real one they had experienced, Latham assured me after the Santa Fe men had withdrawn. But he acknowledged he and the others had been fools for being lulled off their guard.

"How can you trust the word of a drunk in a whorehouse?" was the way he put it. "Especially when he works for the Santa Fe."

Crenshaw, with his strong sense of duty, had elected to stay behind and hold the fort at whatever cost until he got word otherwise from Remmer or General Palmer himself.

It was slow going, since we dared not light a torch. We felt our way along, in single file, keeping close to the rock walls. We approached every bend in the trail as if an enemy was lurking just beyond. We stopped and held our collective breath every time someone's foot kicked a stone. But we heard nothing. The noise of the river next to us muffled any sounds. Once Gil Latham tangled his long legs in some branches of driftwood caught between two rocks and sprawled headlong. His rifle went clattering away. We were several minutes finding the weapon where it had stopped, just short of going into the river.

The moon finally rose above the walls of the Gorge and cast its pale light down inside. It wasn't much, but it was like daylight compared to what we had experienced. Even though we could see the outlines of the rock trail and wall a little better, we were now more visible and vulnerable to anyone who might be guarding the trail out.

But we saw no one, heard no one. Mile followed weary mile as we wound our way down the long canyon. The moon set and cast us into tarlike blackness again. We plodded along, one foot after another, our minds numbed by fatigue and the soporific rushing sounds of the water beside us.

Finally I became aware that I could see a little better. The early dawn light very gradually drew itself up over the edge of the world, as we crawled like ants along a crack in the earth's surface.

By this time we had all been at least twenty-four hours without sleep, and Kerlin and I had already walked several miles into the canyon. At this point, I felt as if I had spent my entire life walking up and down this same rocky trail.

DeArmand, who was leading, put up his hand and stopped.

"Let's take a breather!"

The rest of us were only too glad to oblige as we sank wearily to the ground where we stood. I sat with my back to the rock wall, leaned my head back, and closed my eyes for a few blessed minutes.

I think I must have dozed off, but had no idea how long I had been asleep, when I heard a clank of metal against rock. My eyes flew open, but I never moved my head as I tried to orient myself. The gray morning was a little brighter. I rolled my head slightly to the right. Ex-sergeant Kerlin was staring at me and quickly put his finger to his lips. He had heard it, too. DeArmand and Latham were both asleep, one lying on his side, the other slumped against a boulder, his head pillowed on his crushed hat.

I was wide awake and alert now. The bearded Irishman and I both eased to a crouch and then stood up, taking extreme care not to make a sound. I drew my Colt. He already had his Adams in his big fist.

We had stopped short of a sharply jutting rock ledge that almost blocked the trail and cut off our view within a few feet. A gray, chill early-morning mist hung over the canyon.

A man coughed and spat only a few feet away. I froze, and a chill went up my back. Someone was just around the bend from us. If DeArmand hadn't stopped to rest when he had, we'd have stumbled right into them, whoever they were.

We dared not to take the chance of making any noise by trying to wake our companions, so Kerlin and I, by use of hand signals to each other, prepared to confront whoever it was.

But the gods were against us. As I stepped forward, eyes on the edge of jutting rock, Colt cocked and pointed upward, I miscalculated the size of DeArmand's big foot sprawled across the trail. My toe caught his boot and I pitched forward. I unconsciously squeezed the trigger, and I heard my Colt roar as I fell forward with a curse.

From then on everything was a blur. I vaguely remember seeing Kerlin jump past me and start yelling for someone to throw up their hands. There were yells, and Kerlin's pistol went off with a crash that almost deafened my right ear as I scrambled to my feet. Four dim figures appeared through the smoke. A slug blew a hole in the coffeepot. Hot steam from the fire blinded one man who was charging, head down, at me. He threw his hands to his face and staggered to one side. As I brought up my Colt and cocked it, a stick of firewood slammed my right forearm. My gun went flying and my arm went numb. I grabbed my arm and threw my left shoulder into the midsection of the man who had hit me. He sat down on the fire with a sudden grunt. I backed up a step and had a second or two to look around. The feeling was coming back into my arm, and it hurt like hell. We had caught this bunch by surprise. Two of the four men were just rolling out of their blankets. Kerlin had buffaloed the first man we had surprised cooking breakfast. The one who had shot the coffeepot was just getting to his feet after being scalded by the steam. I aimed a kick at his midsection as he rose. He went down again with a grunt of pain. That left the two just waking up. One was thickset and had several days' growth of black whiskers. He was staggering up, with eyes puffy from sleep. But he caught a heel in the blanket. He bent to free it, and I rushed him. I butted him in the rear end like a charging bull. With a yell of surprise, he pitched forward into the surging current of the Arkansas. I saw an arm and a head bob to the surface before he was swept out of sight around the next bend, his yells lost in the tumult.

I whirled around, and Gil Latham and Greg DeArmand were finally getting into the fray. The odds had more than evened up. The fight was suddenly over. They had their rifles leveled at the three remaining men, who had their hands in the air.

"You could've at least woke us up before all the fireworks started." DeArmand grinned.

"Well, what the hell you gonna do now?" one of our captives growled, his hands still safely in plain sight as he backed away and eyed the four of us. "You prob'ly just drowned Chaz. He don't swim too good."

"At the rate that current's carrying him along, he won't have to swim much."

The three men we had captured were unshaven and roughly dressed. They had been armed with shotguns, I noted, as well as rifles and pistols. I thought how lucky we had been not to encounter any guards on this trail on our hike in. They must have made camp here when they pulled back from yesterday's attack.

The morning light was slowly increasing, and we could see everything plainly now. One of the three men was slender and had straight blond hair and blue eyes. The other two were of average height, but one was thickset and had a receding hairline.

"I asked you what you plan to do with us

now?" the one man repeated, his voice bitter.

"If you boys were supposed to be on guard, you did a mighty poor job of it," Latham said.

In spite of the pain in my forearm, I almost laughed out loud. These men would never know that only sheer luck had prevented us from stumbling into them in the predawn darkness.

"I guess you'll just have to report to your Santa Fe bosses that you let a few of the Rio Grande boys out of your trap," I added, looking around on the rocky ground for my Colt.

The two dark-headed men glanced at each other.

"What makes you think we work for the Santa Fe?" one of them asked.

"Don't you?"

"No," the spokesman replied after a slight hesitation.

"You boys are not only bad guards, you need a little practice lying, too."

"Damn!" DeArmand exclaimed, glancing at the mess on the ground where the cooking fire had been in a small circle of stones. "Somebody plugged the coffeepot. And you know how I am before I've had my morning coffee."

"Disposition like a grizzly with a thorn in his paw," Latham confided to our three captives. The three men were beginning to look a little nervous.

Picking up his cue from this, Kerlin said, "When I was in Her Majesty's forces in the back country of Zululand, we had no bathing facilities, but we were expected to keep clean nonetheless. There were always the rivers to bathe in and wash our uniforms. You gentlemen have a downwind odor that would attract the vultures. And when did you last apply a razor to those cheeks? It would seem that soldiers in the service of the Atchison, Topeka and Santa Fe Railroad should present a more fitting appearance." He glanced suggestively at the river.

I took it up from there. "Seems we could kill two birds with one stone. You three need a bath, and the quickest way out of this canyon is by water. It's only a couple of miles to Canon City. By the time you get there, you'd be nice and clean to make your report to Marshal Bat Masterson."

"Oh, no, you don't!" said the stocky one with the receding hairline, backing away.

Kerlin and I grabbed him by each arm while Latham and DeArmand kept the other two at bay with the Winchesters.

"A refreshing morning dip never hurt anyone," Latham gravely assured him, as the thickset one braced his feet and struggled. With a mighty yank, the two of us jerked him forward and he pitched headfirst with a yell into the swirling current. He came up gasping and cursing. He tried to stroke back to the bank, but the current, which was running a good ten knots or more, swept him toward the opposite bank as the river curved into its next bend. He was still shouting curses at us as he disappeared downstream.

"I can't swim." The blond one spoke up, trying to keep his jaw from quivering.

"Then it's high time you learned. A man of your age should know such things. Here, grab hold of this." DeArmand kicked a fair-sized log loose from the pile of driftwood. The slim man grabbed it just as Kerlin and I heaved him into the river. The cold spray wet us as he splashed in.

The last man took advantage of our distraction to make a run for it. Latham's Winchester cracked and a bullet whined off the rocky ground about two feet in front of him. The man stopped in his tracks. He slowly turned to face the four of us, who were grinning at him.

"You sonsabitches are gonna live to regret this. Dodge City boys don't take kindly to this kind of hoorahing," he snarled. Then he took a deep breath and looked at the river, high, and rolling its frigid cargo along. With a sudden, defiant yell, he took two steps and hurled himself headfirst into it. The splash subsided, but he didn't appear. Then, about five seconds later, he bobbed up several yards downstream, shook a fist at us, and then was swept from view around the bend.

On April twenty-first, the Supreme Court handed down its decision. It ruled that the Denver & Rio Grande had prior right to construction in the Royal Gorge. Even though these nine learned men in Washington had thus ruled, there was much more to the written decision. As to most men of the law, nothing is ever black and white, so they further stipulated that, even though the D&RG had prior rights, it did not have *exclusive* rights, which left the door open for further lawsuits in the lower courts about how to resolve that issue.

But the fine print of the decision did not matter to those on the Colorado frontier. A decision was a decision, and we had won. The fine points of the law be damned. Headlines in the Canon City, Pueblo, Colorado Springs, and Denver newspapers blared the news. Few paused to read past the first paragraph.

The D&RG employees and sympathizers went wild with delight. The celebrations lasted the better part of three days. No one really cared that the trains to and from Denver failed to run on time or that the crews showed up with hangovers. What mattered was that the D&RG would not go out of business or be swallowed up by the big Santa Fe moguls. It meant that General Palmer's little road would now have access to the lucrative business of hauling silver and gold ores out of Leadville and all the other Colorado mining towns tucked away in the fastness of the rugged Rockies. Its future was secured. The decision made General Palmer look like the David who slew the mighty Goliath. Or, at the very least, it made him look like a prophet, in addition to his being a financial genius and a hard-driving, long-visioned business pioneer.

Kerlin, Diego Chavez, and I were respiking some loosened ties and replacing some rotting ties twenty miles north of Pueblo when we got the news from the engineer of a passing freight. We were ready to throw our tools into an empty boxcar and ride on back to town to begin celebrating. But Crenshaw, our foreman, was having none of that. He did unbend enough to tell our gang that if we waited until the end of our shift and rode the handcars back, he would buy all of us the first round of drinks. He was as good as his word.

It was only two days after the decision that Bat Masterson and his carload of hired toughs entrained for Dodge City. According to a newspaper report, Bat was quoted as saying that he was a peace officer, sworn to uphold the law, and could not, in this capacity, advocate violence by ordering his men to attack the strongholds of the Rio Grande men in the Gorge. But the editor surmised that the sight of four of his best guards showing up in Canon City, wet, half-frozen, and disarmed, might have had something to do with his decision not to attack the Rio Grande's heavily fortified positions. And one of these guards, the editor delighted in pointing out, was the notorious Texas badman, Ben Thompson, who had come with Bat Masterson and his boys.

In any event, since the issue had apparently been decided, Bat took his men home, and everyone breathed a sigh of relief. Everyone, that is, except General Palmer, whose road was still under lease to the Santa Fe. He immediately had his lawyers file suit in district court to have the lease broken so that he could get his railroad back. After all, he argued, how could he start building again and begin showing a profit for his bondholders if he didn't have control of his road?

All in all, it was a happy, easy time for me and the friends I had made and shared so much with since I had ridden down from Denver in the snow a few months earlier.

While the wheels of the judicial system were slowly turning in the courts, life went on routinely for the rest of us foot soldiers of the D&RG.

Warm spring weather was advancing quicker than normal along the eastern foot of the Rockies. It wasn't long until most of us elected to move out of the cramped and stuffy boxcar sleeping quarters to find some spots nearby to camp singly or in small groups. We purchased some small tents in Pueblo or on trips up the line to Colorado Springs or Denver. Some were new, others used or surplus of the army. The camp was a hodgepodge of various shelters, overlaid with the smoke of numerous cooking fires in the evenings, even though about half the men still chose to take their meals from the mess car. We had more men than we really needed to get the work done, but the management of the D&RG was reluctant to let anyone go until this matter of control of the road and the Gorge was finally settled. Even though the Supreme Court had declared the D&RG had prior rights to the Royal Gorge, General Palmer could not order any grading or track laying to begin until the lease was broken or set aside and control of the railroad was returned to him. In the meantime, our work gangs alternated assignments. When we weren't working, most of us were lounging around camp, sleeping, gambling, or drinking in Pueblo, or hunting jack-rabbits or antelope in the foothills.

Diego Chavez had returned to work about a week before the Supreme Court decision was handed down on April twenty-first. Frankly, I had despaired of ever seeing him again. He was paler than before and had lost weight. He had dark circles under his eyes. He looked as if he had been sick. Kerlin and I surmised that he had overdone the penances during Holy Week and was taking longer to recover. But we couldn't be sure. We never saw him without his shirt, sleeping or waking. Unlike most white men, he eschewed the wearing of longjohns in the winter. But, as the month of May drew on and grew warmer and warmer, he never shed his shirt, as most of us did while doing hard manual labor in the hot sun. We paid the price with the intense late spring sun on the white skins of our backs, but I don't believe Chavez was worried about sunburn, since he was already considerably darker than the rest of us. We felt sure it was to hide the recently healed scars of a severe lashing. When he first returned to us, he had little to say but was quiet and friendly just as before. However, he took little part in any card playing or entertainment that Kerlin and I indulged in. Instead, for the first few days, he asked if he might borrow my horse almost daily to take a ride until he could get his first paycheck and afford to rent a mount. I readily agreed but was curious. He never said where he was going and always rode off by himself toward the mountains. He always put a small sack into the saddlebags, which I assumed was something to eat. Kerlin and I discussed it and came to the conclusion that these rides were to build up his strength and to get himself some fresh air and exercise.

But this was not the purpose of the rides. He returned one night after dark, unsaddled my bay, rubbed him down, and picketed him to graze about a quarter mile from our tent. Then he went straight to his bedroll and turned in. It was an unusually warm night for late April, and shortly he had kicked his blanket off. Kerlin and I were playing poker on an upturned box by the light of a coal-oil lamp that hung from the ridgepole of our wall tent. Chavez began to moan and thrash around in his sleep. There was nothing unusual about this, since he usually had very vivid dreams, he had told us. But when it continued for some time, I got up to check on him. He was wearing a sleeveless white cotton undershirt, which was also his habit. But when he rolled over on his stomach, I saw the shirt was all blotched from top to waist with a brown, bloody serum. The shirt was virtually glued to his back with half-healed scabs. There was a strange odor emanating from him, which I finally identified.

"Carbolic. No need to wonder where he's been going every day," I remarked to Kerlin, who had gotten up to stand beside me as we looked at the sleeping man. "I'll bet he rides off to some deserted arroyo to treat and disinfect those back wounds himself so nobody will see him."

He nodded. "I have no sympathy for him.

Any man who would do that to himself deserves all the pain he gets."

"Think we should offer to help him in the morning?"

He shook his head firmly as he resumed his seat by the box to continue our game. "You would be trying to alleviate the pain that he purposely brought on himself."

"No, I would only be trying to disinfect the wounds so no severe complications might result. In fact, I'd probably make them sting worse with alcohol or carbolic."

"Whatever you fancy." He shrugged. "He's obviously balmy."

But the next morning, even though I broached the subject carefully, the young man rejected my offer immediately without a word of thanks or even admitting the cause of the seeping wounds. He brushed me off as if it were nothing to be concerned about. That day we were called out to fix the timber supports of a small bridge whose underpinnings had been loosened and nearly washed out. Diego Chavez pulled his weight and more in helping shift the heavy timbers and respiking them in place. And all the while he wore a heavy blue woolen shirt, even though sweat was pouring from his face and the shirt was stained even darker with it.

"Ach! Salt in the wounds. I'm sure he loves every bit of it!" Kerlin snorted when we took a water break about midafternoon. "What a blinking idiot! What a masochist! We had a man like that once in my outfit in Durban. He was summarily dismissed from the service. Men who love pain are not normal!" He flung the rest of the water away and replaced the dipper in the bucket.

"They're not normal if they love pain for its own sake," I said quietly. "Or if they derive some sort of perverse pleasure from it." Then I grabbed my shovel and moved off quickly before he could respond.

But Chavez struggled along and gradually healed and recovered his strength. It was amazing to see him eat. Once he began to mend in earnest, I marveled at the amount he could eat. It was as if his body were sucking up the energy from the food and turning it into solid, wholesome flesh. He grew stronger day by day, and the circles disappeared from his eyes. And work! He volunteered for the hardest tasks. He always wanted to be a spiker whenever any rails had to be laid or ties replaced, even though our foreman preferred to assign this job to the biggest and strongest of our crew. Swinging a spiking sledge seemed to suit him fine. And he quickly got to the point where he could drive a spike into a solid tie with only three strokes. A considerable feat, I discovered when I tried it myself. I had heard of track layers on the first Union Pacific and elsewhere who were eventually able to drive a spike routinely with only two mighty blows, but these men were more the exception than the rule. And Chavez rebounded from his self-torture like a leaping mountain lion. His face and arms were a deep bronze from the early summer sun. His shoulders and arms and neck gradually swelled with muscle.

He was not just the young man I had met in February; he was more. With his dark eyes and hair, straight nose, and smooth, flat cheeks, he was very handsome. But he never went to town with the two of us or any of the other men. Nor did he seem interested in associating with the other Spanish-speaking laborers who worked for the D&RG. He never mentioned having seen us at his village during Holy Week — that is, if he had been there himself. We certainly had not identified him. It seemed I knew less about this loner than when I had first met him. He was an enigma to me and I'm sure to Mike Kerlin as well.

But one night when Kerlin and I were returning on foot from Pueblo to our camp about a mile away, we saw Chavez. He was coming down the steps of the fanciest parlor house in Pueblo. And he was obviously drunk, judging from the careful way he walked.

"Hey, Diego! Wait a minute!" I yelled at him. "Where ya headed?"

He looked quickly in our direction, and then turned abruptly and started back toward downtown at a fast walk, without answering.

Kerlin looked at me and silently shook his head. I said nothing, but I somehow felt let down.

"Hypocrite" was all Mike Kerlin said. I felt the urge to defend Chavez, but while I searched for the appropriate words, the moment passed. So I said nothing. Mike Kerlin, the transplanted Irishman, and I had two common bonds that made us think much alike — our basic religious beliefs and a shared homeland. But something — perhaps his military background — prevented him from being tolerant of divergent points of view. So anything I might say in favor of Diego Chavez, I was sure, would probably fall on deaf ears. Better to let things go and stay out of it for now, I decided. Let him think what he wanted. I would just act as a peacemaker should any open conflict ensue. At least Kerlin had made no move toward trying to oust Chavez from being our tentmate.

The seasons slowly evolved, and the month of May faded into June and a hot, dry, early summer. And still no word came from the courts about returning the D&RG to General Palmer's control.

One hot noonday toward the end of the first week of the month, we were returning to camp after helping unload a carload of foodstuffs in Pueblo when a rider came galloping in, slid his mount to a stop in a cloud of dust, and hit the ground running, waving a paper in his hand.

"Hey, listen to this! Telegram just in from Remmer at Colorado Springs!"

Men came running from various tents and

the mess car. The courier hesitated until most of us were within earshot. "Says here that W. B. Strong, the head of the Santa Fe, has called in Bat Masterson and a bunch of his gunhands from Dodge City again. Ben Thompson and Doc Holliday are with them. And about forty-five men from Trinidad who've been deputized."

"What the hell for?" somebody shouted. "Has the court come down with some decision?"

"No. This telegram just came over the wire not ten minutes ago, and it says that Strong expects a decision any time, and he knows it's going against him, so he's getting his forces together to keep us from getting our road back, no matter what the court says."

"Hell, that don't make no sense," another voice said. "The Santa Fe's a big outfit. They can't just turn outlaw all of a sudden."

"They did it about two months ago and defied the courts!" another man said.

"Wait. Wait. There's more," the courier said, holding up his hand. "Remmer goes on to say that Strong wants to hold the status quo until he has time to file a counter suit in court as soon as the decision comes down to restore our road. Strong's afraid General Palmer will try to take the D and RG back by force before the Santa Fe can get to court and block the move again. Strong's sure he can have the order reversed."

“Damn! If this thing gets any more complicated, they’re gonna have to draw me a picture,” somebody said.

“Why don’t they let these lawyers shoot it out and then the rest of us will abide by the results?” a big man next to me yelled. There was a general chuckle that eased the tension.

“How does Carl Remmer know what W. B. Strong at the Santa Fe is thinking?” I asked. “Does he have spies inside their offices?”

The courier shrugged. “All I know is what this telegram says. Maybe he tapped their telegraph messages. Anyway, he’s warning us to be ready to defend railroad property at a moment’s notice. He says he’ll keep us informed of developments.”

The courier stuffed the telegram into his shirt pocket and remounted his horse.

Crenshaw had been called away to Colorado Springs two days before, along with the three other foremen from our camp. I thought nothing of it at the time, but, in light of what we had just heard, I began to wonder if it might have had something to do with the crisis that was shaping up.

We were not long in finding out. Late that afternoon, the regular passenger train pulled in from the north and, as the engine slowed, the four foremen dropped off the step of the first passenger coach. In spite of the fact that it was the supper hour, they gathered their men around them.

Kerlin, Chavez, and I crowded up to the stocky Crenshaw. His serious face was even grimmer than usual.

"Boys, I heard you got the telegraph message Carl Remmer sent down earlier today," he began with no preliminaries. "I'm sure you're wondering what's going on. There's really no need for you to know everything that's been happening for the past few weeks. But General Palmer thinks of all of you as family. And he wants every one of you to be aware of what he's been doing and what we're up against. That's the reason he called all the foremen and the two section bosses to his office in Colorado Springs. I had heard some rumors earlier that General Palmer was preparing to take his road back from the Santa Fe by force if the courts didn't act, or if Mr. Strong, chief operations officer of the Santa Fe, didn't agree to break the lease. Well, I found out the rumors were correct. During May the general was lining up some arms and preparing for the worst. At South Pueblo here we have a box of rifles and thirteen pistols. At the El Moro coke ovens on south of here, we have six rifles and six Colt revolvers. From Walsenburg, the company has ten rifles and six .45-caliber pistols. Just a few days ago, on June fifth, General Palmer telegraphed Carl Remmer here in Pueblo that additional guns were on their way by wagon — thirty pistols and twenty carbines with ammunition . . ."

"Bud Risley, the telegraph operator in town, is a staunch Santa Fe man." One of the men in our group spoke up. "I've had a few drinks with him, and he makes no bones about his loyalties. How can he be trusted to handle messages like that? You can be damn sure everybody in the Santa Fe camp knows what's going on, too."

"They might and they might not," Crenshaw answered, digging a fistful of papers out of his jacket pocket. "These here messages are coded. He might suspect that something was up, but he wouldn't know the details. Here, I copied some down. Let me read one." He selected a crinkled sheet and smoothed it out. " 'New page flesh affable caliber. No bemoan wad tempest.' Anybody care to translate that? No? Well, it means, 'New pistols, .44 caliber. No ammunition with them.' So you can see the general has been gearing up for trouble. He knows W. B. Strong and the Santa Fe management. He's not about to let us get caught with our pants down while we wait on another court decision. Besides, he hinted to us at the meeting that there might be a little bribery going on to influence the judge's decision. He said we had to be ready for anything. Since he expects a favorable decision any day from Judge Bowen at Alamosa, he's directing that our men be armed and dropped off at all the D and RG stations along the line from Denver to Colorado Springs to Pueblo to Canon City and all points in between. The Santa Fe people know something's coming, so they're doing all they can to disrupt our communication. They've chopped down the telegraph poles between Florence and our coal mines. Also between Canon City and Colorado Springs. The general has wired Governor Frederick Pitkin to complain about this interruption of public information over the wires. Until the wires can be repaired, or a courier rides through, we can't get the message about the decision from Judge Thomas Bowen of the Fourth Judicial District at Alamosa. General Palmer told us that he had heard in a roundabout way that the judge had already handed down an order for the Santa Fe to release our road back to us, but that the court clerk could not be found to affix his seal to the order, so that it wasn't yet legal. But it's also rumored that the clerk has been bought off by the enemy."

He stuffed the papers back into his pocket. "So there you have it, men. At last count the general told us we had two hundred and seven Colt pistols and two hundred and fifty-nine rifles at our disposal, not counting what you boys may own yourselves. You've already got the word that the Santa Fe is sending in more men than before, so it looks like a showdown is coming in the next couple of days. We'll be split up and dropped off at points all along the line to be ready to take and hold all the D and RG depots as soon as the judge rules. They won't block us this time with any guns or legal maneuvers. By God, we'll take what's ours!"

A spontaneous cheer went up from our group.

"Be ready to move out tonight. A train will be going north within the hour."

My stomach tensed at the thought of battle. But I was also excited at the prospect. I wanted to get this thing resolved once and for all, after the months and years the conflict had dragged on. Kerlin had a calm, ex-soldier's face, and Chavez was as impassive as usual. What were they thinking? I wondered as the group broke up. How many men might lose their lives making sure General Palmer's "little road" would survive?

The huge round headlamp of the locomotive poured its brightness along the shining rails as the train slowed, then ground to a halt in a hiss of steam.

It was an hour later and full dark. Gil Latham, the lanky engineer, swung down from the footplate of the Rio Bravo, a 4-4-0, Baldwin-built locomotive that had been in service only a year.

"Matt, we hooked on two stock cars for the horses," he greeted me, jerking a thumb over his shoulder.

"Good. I want to have my bay close by. May not need him, but then again . . ."

I led my horse toward the rear of the short train that had stopped on the siding parallel to our camp. Kerlin and Chavez brought their rented saddle mounts up at the same time. The three of us had decided that we were going to be prepared for anything. Or, rather, Kerlin and I had decided to bring horses, and Chavez had silently gone along as well. The shod hooves clattered hollowly on the wooden ramp as we led the animals up into the slat-sided cars. The floor had been thickly strewn with fresh straw, reasonably comfortable traveling arrangements for the eight horses we put in it. Another identical car just behind it held about a dozen horses. Only about half the men entraining felt it necessary, or had the means on short notice, to bring a mount. We had no clear idea of what to expect. We had been given only the vaguest of instructions. The wires were crackling up and down the line from Denver to Pueblo. All we knew was that we were to go north to Denver as fast as possible, and should be ready to secure all D&RG property — depot, offices, rolling stock, everything. Men were being rushed to every station along the line to do the same.

The decision had not even come down from District Judge Bowen in Alamosa to negate the lease and return control of the Rio Grande to General Palmer, but both sides were rushing to get into position — one to keep the road, and one to take it back by force, if necessary. Both were anticipating the same decision by the judge, who was basically following the Supreme Court. That August body had ruled the Rio Grande had prior rights to the Gorge. But it had also decreed that we did not have exclusive rights, and passed the buck back to a lower court to decide the thorny issue of how to allow parallel trackage in parts of the Gorge that were wide enough and joint trackage in those parts that were too narrow for more than one set of narrow-gauge rails.

But we were not concerned about these arguments at the moment. We had been instructed by our employers to defend what we all thought of as our property. There was no question in our minds as to the right or wrong of it. On that we were all agreed.

It was a silent crowd that piled aboard the passenger coaches. This was no group of common laborers traveling in boxcars. This time we were concerned employees, traveling well armed on the padded benches of the passenger coaches. We were defenders of the right and of our jobs. I had the feeling that this time no one would be using blanks.

The train started with a sudden jolt and I had to grab the back of a seat to keep from being thrown off my feet as I swung myself down beside Kerlin, who sat next to the window. We rolled over the siding switch and north onto the main line. It was only a few minutes before the jerking and swaying of the car told me Latham was not holding back. The wheels clicked over the rail joints with the rhythm and speed of a telegrapher's key.

As I glanced around at the men who filled the car, I read a variety of moods in their faces. The overhead oil lamps had been dimmed slightly, and the hats of some shielded their faces in shadow. But of those I could see some were tight-lipped, grim. Others were talking or joking quietly with their seatmates. Two or three had their hats tipped over their eyes and appeared to be dozing. Maybe they were the smart ones. They were going to get some rest while they could. It might prove to be a long night.

Chavez sat across the aisle and back two seats. He had made no attempt to sit near us, as the invisible barrier between him and Mike Kerlin was still in place. In fact, I think if it hadn't been for me, Kerlin would have booted him out of our tent. What Chavez was thinking at this moment, or at any time, was a matter for conjecture since his handsome face was always impassive.

Just over an hour later we reached Colorado Springs. The locomotive drew to a halt in a cloud of steam and stood panting after the fast run north. Kerlin and I slipped off onto the platform from the forward end of the car. We joined Crenshaw and several other men who trooped off up the street toward the frame building that General Palmer used for his headquarters.

"You men get back on the train! We'll be leavin' in a few minutes!" Crenshaw yelled, trying to wave back the stream of men who swarmed up the street after him and the other foremen. But to no avail. We all pounded up the steps behind him and shouldered our way into the room that served as part office, part living quarters. A big, coal-oil lamp spread a large pool of light over a massive wooden desk in the middle of the room. The desk was covered with papers, and a telegrapher hunched over a key behind the desk. He was in shirtsleeves. Above the green eyeshade, his thinning hair was in wild disarray.

"Welcome, gentlemen!" A man I recognized from his photographs as General Palmer stepped from behind the telegrapher's shoulder and came toward us. "You made good time. Gil Latham was at the throttle, I'll wager."

The founder and driving force of the D&RG and the reason all of us were there was a slim man, erect, with sandy hair and mustache. He was in shirtsleeves and vest. A gold watch chain stitched together the pockets of his vest. His blue eyes picked out each of our faces in turn.

"Some of you already know Carl Remmer," Palmer said, indicating a third man in the room. "My good right arm."

Remmer was a broad-shouldered man with a square-jawed face and coal-black hair. He nodded curtly to the two dozen or so of us who were crowded into the room.

The telegraph key began to chatter, and the rumpled man hunched over the desk and began scribbling on a pad.

The slight smile faded from Palmer's face as he hurried over to the desk to look again over the shoulder of his telegrapher. He seemed to forget the rest of us for a minute as the two of them worked on the message.

Finally he looked up. "We've tapped the line and are intercepting messages from the Santa Fe forces," he explained. "It's coded, but we've had no trouble breaking it. This message was going to Denver. It seems that a trainload of men from Trinidad has just arrived in Pueblo. Some of them are leaving immediately for Canon City. We've already found out that another train will be headed this way before daylight with about sixty Santa Fe men aboard."

"The court hasn't even ruled yet, General," Crenshaw said.

"Wrong. Less than an hour ago a courier rode in from Alamosa with the news that Judge Bowen has ruled just like everyone thought he would. The wires are cut between here and Canon City, so the message had to be carried by horseback."

General Palmer came around the desk again and faced us.

"I've telegraphed the sheriffs up and down the line from Denver to Pueblo of the court's decision and asked their help in defending our company property from impending attack. Even now I'm receiving replies that they're deputizing men to help. By daybreak, they should be preparing to move in on most of the stations up and down the line." He leaned back against the desk and held out his arms as if to embrace the lot of us who had crowded into the room. "Here's what I want you men to do.

Run up to Denver as fast as you can. Be ready to lend a hand to any sheriff who needs your help. Start at Denver. I don't think anyone will have time to make a move before you get there. The company's main administrative offices are in west Denver. They must be secured at all costs. They must not fall into the enemy's hands. We have the full power of the law behind us in this. Use force only if you have to, but don't hesitate if it's necessary. I know you men are not soldiers, but you're gritty. And I know you won't let anyone run over you. Seizing and retaining all of the D and RG property is our main objective here. All of our futures are at stake!"

Two short blasts on the steam whistle galvanized us into action. Crenshaw stayed behind to say something to Palmer as the rest of us crowded out the door and ran for the train.

We had barely gotten inside the coach when the train gave a lurch and we were in motion. Crenshaw had not yet shown up. As the train gathered speed, Kerlin cupped his hands to the dark glass beside him.

"I don't see him."

I leaned across him and looked. Then I saw something moving far back. "There he is." The short legs were pumping furiously as he chased the red lantern of the caboose. "Come on. . . . Come on. . . ." He made a lunge for the last platform and caught hold. His feet were dragging, but then some helping arms pulled him aboard past my sight.

"He made it," Kerlin sighed, leaning back in his seat.

As I sat back I felt the unaccustomed lump of my holstered Colt on my hip. My hand went to it automatically. The loops in my gun belt were filled with fresh .44 cartridges supplied by the railroad. Kerlin had been supplied with the same ammunition, but he preferred to carry his Adams instead of a company Colt. "It's seen me through the devil's own hell before, and I'll trust it again," he had said, when offered another gun.

Neither of us carried a rifle or carbine, not feeling the need for a longer-range weapon. Diego Chavez, who seldom went armed even though he owned a revolver, sat across the aisle from us, cradling a short, double-barreled shotgun, the side pockets of his short canvas coat filled with loose 12-gauge shells. His Colt was belted underneath.

I wondered if we would really need all this firepower. But it was better to be prepared for anything. I leaned back and closed my eyes. But it was next to impossible to doze off, even though it was a little past midnight and I'd already put in a long day. Kerlin, whose bearded chin protruded from under his hat beside me, appeared to be asleep. The clicking of the wheels and the swaying of the dimly lighted car normally would have lulled me into a doze. But not tonight. I was too keyed up. At the rate we seemed to be moving, I estimated we would pull into the Denver depot in an hour or so.

I don't remember going to sleep, but suddenly I was wide awake as my left cheek and shoulder slammed into the back of the seat in front of me. The shrill screeching of brakes and the sound of metal against metal assaulted my ears as I tumbled out into the aisle. The car was in an uproar as the sudden deceleration continued for long seconds in the screeching of metal. Then I felt a jolt travel through the train. The car tilted and I felt the wheels bumping along the ties as we derailed. The car rocked up and then several of the right-side windows burst inward in a shower of glass and dirt. We ground to a halt with the coach tilted at a crazy angle.

For a second or two there was silence. Then several men were shouting at once as we untangled ourselves from the floor, the seats, and each other.

"Get out that rear end and see what happened!"

"Can't. The door's jammed!"

Kerlin was already at the forward door. It was also sprung, but he managed to get it open a few inches. Then he backed off and slammed his booted foot at the door. It didn't move. Once again. The glass in the door window was shivered, but the door was open far enough for us to squeeze out. Chavez and I were right behind Kerlin. We nearly fell off the platform, it was tilted so far over. We stumbled to our feet to find that the wooden coach was resting on its side against the grassy bank of a cut, which was the only thing that had prevented it from going all the way over. The passenger coach behind us had been pulled over, but only its forward end was resting against the bank. Luckily, the two stock cars and the caboose were still upright, but off the rails.

The coupling had snapped between the tender and our coach. The locomotive and tender both lay on their sides. They bulked black and shiny in the moonlight with steam rising, as from some giant, prehistoric, overheated elephant. I couldn't react. Kneeling there on the grass on one knee, I felt dull-witted, slow, as I tried to focus my mind. Was I still half asleep? Or had I taken too hard a whack on the face when I was flung into the seat ahead of me? My swelling cheekbone was tender when I put my hand to it.

"What the hell happened?" a man yelled.

"Thought we'd been attacked," another man shouted.

"Naw. We were just goin' too damn fast and jumped the tracks," another replied.

"Look to the horses! Make sure none of 'em bust a leg or sumpin'. That was one helluva jolt."

Several men ran toward the stock cars, where hooves were thudding on the wooden floors of the cars and the horses were snorting and whinnying in fear.

"Matt! Matt!"

Kerlin's voice cut through the haze in my

brain. I looked up dully.

"The engineer. The stoker." He signaled for me to follow him. I pushed to my feet and staggered after him, my legs feeling stiff and disjointed on the uneven ground.

The big Irishman leapt, nimble as a cat, over the wet ground, where the water from the overturned tank had soaked the grass. He bounded over the pile of spilled coal and landed on the upper side of the cab.

"Gil! DeArmand! Where are you?" he shouted, poking his head down through the side window. The only answer was the loud hissing of steam.

I pulled myself up to the vertical roof of the cab and crawled inside. The fire door was ajar, casting a dull glow.

"They're not here, Mike," I said quietly, my head beginning to clear somewhat.

"Where's Latham?" one of the men shouted, running up to help.

"Musta jumped before the wreck."

"Gawd! They could be flattened under this thing."

"Matt . . ."

The sound of my name came weakly during a few seconds of silence. The voice was almost a whisper, and a chill went up my back as I looked around quickly.

"Matt . . ." the voice said again, slightly stronger this time.

"Over here!" I jumped down and started toward a dark lump that was barely moving. "Damn! Wish we had a torch. Anybody got a lantern?"

The lump on the grass several yards from the wrecked locomotive turned out to be Gil Latham.

"How bad you hurt, Gil?" I asked, squatting beside him and sliding an arm under his shoulders.

"Think I broke my ankle when I hit. A rib, too, maybe. I hit pretty hard."

"Your head and neck okay?"

"Yeah. Jarred me. Kinda stunned. Think I was out for a minute or two."

"Where's DeArmand?"

"Dunno. He jumped on the other side."

I eased him to a sitting position. The tall engineer caught his breath and put a hand to his side. Kerlin and four other men grouped around. I didn't see Chavez.

"What happened, Gil?"

"Somebody yanked a rail out. Didn't see it in time. My fault. Going too fast. Couldn't get 'er stopped."

"Santa Fe men must have known we were coming and got here in time to derail us," one of the men said bitterly.

"We've gotta find DeArmand," I said, straightening up.

"We need to get away from this engine," Gil Latham said weakly. "That boiler could blow any second."

Without a word, Kerlin carefully scooped the injured man up under his knees and shoulders and gingerly stepped away up the tracks with him. The rest of us followed. He carried him nearly a half mile before the engineer signaled the pain was too much and he had to be put down.

"Somebody needs to go find DeArmand," I said again.

"A couple o' the boys are off after him now," Kerlin answered.

I could hear the yells and hollow drumming of hooves as the horses were being hurriedly unloaded from the two stock cars.

"Matt Latham motioned for me to come closer. I bent down to hear him better where he sat on the ground, holding his ribs.

"Matt, this line's blocked for at least a day or more. The train that's behind us with the Santa Fe men can't get past. When they get here, they'll have to back up all the way to Colorado Springs or Pueblo."

Crenshaw had come up a few minutes earlier and stood close by, listening to the engineer.

"That's right," he interjected. "And General Palmer told me there was a good-sized force of men with the sheriff there, planning to come down on the Santa Fe men at dawn."

"Shall we ride north to help out at Denver?"

Crenshaw pondered the situation for a minute. "No. I think we'd better go back. If this trainload of reinforcements behind us can't get through and has to go back, we'll all be needed to help fight them. They'll surely try to take over the Pueblo roundhouse. The general himself may be in danger in Colorado Springs."

"Even backing up, their train will be faster than our horses," I objected.

"All we can do is try. C'mon, let's get to our horses!"

He churned away from us in short, choppy strides. Six or seven of the men who were standing there followed him.

"Matt!"

I turned back to Latham.

"There may be a faster way."

"What's that?"

"About six miles back we passed a place called Ironwood. It's not a town. Just a siding with some storage sheds, a water tank, and a watchman's shack. A work train is kept there. A small engine and a tender and a few flat cars for maintenance work. If you and Kerlin and DeArmand could ride there and get that engine fired up . . ."

"Hell, you're in no shape to ride."

He shook his head. "That's not what I meant. You can do it."

"Me? You're crazy. I don't know anything about running a locomotive."

"Look, you can do it. If DeArmand's okay, take him with you. He can fire it for you."

"I can't do it."

"I'll give you some quick instructions."

"There's no way I can remember them."

"Then I hope your horses can carry you thirty miles in a mighty short time."

I hesitated. "Okay. It's worth a try. Give it to me slowly, so Kerlin can hear it, too."

BBBOOOOMMMM!!!

All of us went facedown as a ripping explosion shredded the side of the overturned locomotive. For the next half minute, shards of metal, large and small, rained down all around us.

The three-quarter moon was setting when we pulled our horses to a stop at the Ironwood siding. Our mounts and our moonlight ran out at nearly the same time. I don't think the animals would have made another mile. So far, the four of us had been lucky. Even though we had run our horses along the graded roadbed as much as possible, and we had the advantage of bright moonlight, it was still a very chancy thing. Any of our horses could have stepped into a prairie dog hole or an uneven washout and broken a leg and thrown us.

Chavez and I arrived first, with Kerlin, only an average rider, bringing up the rear a half mile back with the slightly injured DeArmand. Our stoker had been found semiconscious with a twisted knee and a gash on his scalp from grazing the edge of a rock.

I pulled the saddle off and led my lathered bay toward the low cottonwood-log watchman's shack. I had a gut feeling that the shack would be empty. I was right. A solid padlock secured the stout wooden door. I was debating whether to fashion some sort of hobbles for my horse when Chavez interrupted my thoughts.

"Matt, I think my horse has gone lame."

"Stone bruise, maybe. Could've picked up a small rock. A lot of ballast along those tracks."

"There is a corral. But some of the poles have fallen down."

"No matter. With your horse lame and mine pretty well blown, they won't be wandering off. Pull that saddle off and we'll turn 'em into it."

Chavez's horse had gotten away in the wild stampede and confusion of opening the stock cars. It had taken him some time to catch his horse. The blast had killed one of our men and injured two horses when the flying jagged metal had caught them. Several men were nursing minor injuries from the wreck as well.

Not all of the men on the train had provided themselves with mounts, and the blast had spooked the rest of the horses that hadn't been caught. So most of the men were stranded on foot and forced to stay behind. They would take care of Gil Latham and guard what was left of the wreck should the train carrying the sixty Santa Fe men show up. I couldn't figure out why someone would derail us. If that someone were on the side of the Santa Fe, the wreck would also prevent their own train from reaching Denver. Either it was some private citizens who were Santa Fe sympathizers or some Santa Fe employees who didn't know what was going on and thought they were helping their cause. In all the confusion of a night operation like this, there were bound to be mixups. Kerlin had noted that when our engine jumped the tracks and overturned, it had taken down a telegraph pole, snapping the line. So, for the time, there would be no communication to the north.

Just as we got our exhausted horses into the broken-down pole corral, DeArmand and Kerlin rode up. The big fireman was leaning over his saddle horn, obviously in pain.

"That little Mexican could have put himself to good use by staying back to help instead of showing us all how he could be the queen's own acrobatic horseman," Kerlin said disgustedly as he dismounted. We helped the big stoker off his horse. With an arm around each of our shoulders, he hobbled toward the locomotive and tender that loomed a little blacker in the darkness.

Chavez busied himself taking care of the horses.

It took both of us boosting him from underneath to get the big man into the cab of the mogul engine. The six drive wheels of the freight locomotive were not as tall as the four drive wheels of the American-type Rio Bravo engine we had just wrecked. But this engine was built for power rather than speed.

With a bad leg, DeArmand would probably be little help at firing. But I insisted that he come, even though he had had to be supported in the saddle. If he weren't too addled from the head blow, he could just sit in the cab and instruct us on how to lay and maintain a decent fire that would get up the proper steam pressure and keep it. If I could remember Latham's instructions, we could get this train rolling — somehow.

The locomotive was kept in a state of readiness. The tender was full of coal, and the tank was topped off with water. I wouldn't have to waste time trying to position it under the nearby water tank.

I fished in my coat pocket and found a block of matches, broke off one and struck it on the nearest iron. By its weak, flickering flare, we found a can of coal oil.

Holding a blood-splotched handkerchief to the side of his head, as he half lay on the stoker's seat box, DeArmand began telling us how to build a fire.

The thudding of hooves announced the approach of riders. My heart jumped as I yanked my Colt and thrust my head out the right side of the cab. With the fire beginning to flare up behind me, I suddenly realized I made a good target and jerked back behind the iron shield of the cab.

"Hello, the train!" one of the horsemen shouted as they milled to a stop a few rods away. "How about a ride? We've just about run our horses into the ground."

I recognized the voice of Sam Anderson, one of the men who had been on the train with us. With a sigh of relief, I holstered my gun and swung down to greet them.

"Step down and turn your horses into that corral over there." As near as I could determine in the dark, there were about a dozen riders. "Where's the rest o' the men?" I knew we had loaded over twenty horses.

"Scattered to hell and gone between here and Denver, I expect," a voice answered. "Had to shoot two horses who broke their legs in the wreck. A couple others hit by flyin' metal. The ones we didn't have aholt of run off in every direction when that boiler let go."

I already knew what had happened, but I wanted to keep the rider talking to make sure this was the voice of Sam Anderson I was hearing and these dark forms with him were friendly riders.

Amid the sounds of winded horses blowing came grunts and squeaking saddle leather as the men dismounted.

Diego Chavez materialized at my elbow. "I unsaddled our horses and turned them out to graze. There is much grass in that big corral."

"*Gracias, amigo.* Would you show these men where it is. It's blacker than the inside of a coal scuttle since that moon went down."

"*Sí.* But it will be getting light in about an hour."

Sam Anderson, whose voice I had recognized, came up to me, leading his horse. He looked closely. "That you, Matt? Thought so. Do you know what the hell's going on? All I'm gettin' is wild rumors." Anderson was an open, friendly man, big and rawboned. He wasn't afraid of the devil himself.

Before I could even reply, my ears caught a far-off sound. I was instantly alert. I strained to sort out the sound from the noises of horses and men around me. It was a quiet, windless night. I walked away a few steps without answering Anderson and cocked my ears again. Was it what I thought? Yes. The sound was faint but unmistakable. It was an approaching locomotive. It had to be the train from Pueblo carrying the Santa Fe men. Palmer had said one was following us north toward Denver and would probably arrive before daylight. Our wreck had effectively blocked the tracks in that direction. I wondered, as the chuffing of the engine grew louder, if the red lantern was still burning on the rear of our caboose six miles north. If not, there could be another wreck, judging from the speed the train appeared to be traveling.

I walked quickly back to Anderson. "Here's the story. That train coming is carrying about sixty well-armed Santa Fe men. As soon as they find the tracks blocked, they'll be backing up as fast as they can, back toward Pueblo. How many men are with you?"

"Nine others."

"That makes fourteen of us altogether, including DeArmand, and he's hurt. Those Santa Fe gunmen outnumber us about four to one. We need to get this engine fired up and get out on the main line behind them. We have to block them from getting back to Colorado Springs or Pueblo to do any damage. As soon as they see our wreck, they're gonna come bustin' back this way as fast as that engine will run in reverse. We've got to get out on that track and stop them. Or at least try to slow them down. Prevent them from getting back south to reinforce the rest of their men who are probably trying to take the Pueblo roundhouse and the depot and office at Colorado Springs."

"Reckon they've got horses with them, like we did?" Anderson asked.

"We'll see in a minute," I said as the sound of the locomotive grew louder. "Hey, you men! Get down out of sight!"

Anderson and I waved to the others, who hustled over to the protection of the engine and tender just as the headlight of the approaching train lanced up the track toward us, swept over the water tank, the shed, the corral, the engine and cars on the siding and was gone as they roared on by.

Looking between the engine and the tender, I saw the train was composed of locomotive, tender, two passenger coaches, and caboose. No livestock cars. No horses. Wherever the men inside those coaches went, they would have to go by train or on foot.

"Reckon they saw us?" Anderson asked.

"I doubt it. If they saw anything, it was the horses. They may or may not make anything of that. The lights in the coaches were dim. They may have been asleep. They're not slowing down, anyway," I added as the acrid coal smoke drifted over us and the red lantern of the caboose quickly shrank in the distance to the clicking of wheels.

"How's that steam coming?" I yelled up at the cab.

Kerlin looked out the side window. "It will be a bit yet."

"How long?"

"At least twenty minutes," I heard DeArmand's weak voice reply.

"Get a move on. We've got to get out of here before they come back."

"Can't rush it, Matt," came the big stoker's voice again. "She's heatin' up as fast as this fire can heat 'er.

"Might be a good idea to hitch up one o' these flat cars," Anderson suggested.

"Right. Easier for all to ride. And we might need it later, who knows?"

"Matt, we should perhaps break the lock from the cabin and get the tools inside." Diego Chavez's voice was close.

It was something I hadn't even considered. "Good idea. We may have to tear up some track to slow them down. Let's go."

Hammering the padlock off with a rock proved as fruitless as trying to pry the hasp away from the wood.

"Stand back."

My Colt roared twice, and the mangled pieces of the lock went flying. By a flickering match, we located a coal-oil lamp on a shelf. With its light we gathered up several crowbars, three pairs of clamps for lifting and carrying rails, a small wooden keg of spikes, a half dozen shovels, a coil of heavy wire, several sledgehammers, and a few other odds and ends, most of which we had no idea we'd ever use.

With many willing hands, we lugged the tools to the flatcar parked behind the tender and piled them aboard. Then we loosened the brake wheels at either end of the car and rolled it forward and coupled it to the back of the tender. A large stack of new ties lined the siding near the tool shack. As an afterthought, I said to Anderson, "Might want to load a few of those ties. That flatcar doesn't offer any protection from bullets."

Without a word, he yelled for three men by name and started for the pile of rough-cut lumber.

Even after all this, the steam was still not up in the engine.

"How much longer?" I yelled up at Kerlin and DeArmand.

Nobody answered.

I grabbed the handrails and swung myself up

to look in the cab. DeArmand was stretched out full length on his back. Kerlin was crouched over him, wiping his face with a wet bandanna.

"What happened?"

"Unconscious. I fear he has a concussion."

"We've got to wake him up and keep him awake."

Anderson had climbed up behind me. He and Kerlin splashed water in the fireman's face and yelled his name over and over.

A sudden whistling of the steam cocks told me maximum pressure had been reached. I stood and looked closely at the gauge to confirm this. I swung open the iron fire door. The glare of the flames was blinding. I let the door clang shut.

"Matt!" The low, urgent voice of Chavez startled me. His head was showing above the edge of the footplate.

"What is it?"

His breath came quickly as if he had been running.

"There is a train coming. Quickly." He pointed north.

"Damn! Get everyone aboard. Now!"

Diego's head disappeared as he dropped to the ground.

I looked around. "Let's go. We've got to move. They're coming back. We've got to get out ahead of them."

Anderson and Kerlin were still working on

DeArmand, who was coming around, but he was still groggy. They had him sitting up with his back leaning against the opposite seat.

I leaned out the left side. The distant wail of a steam whistle came to my ears on the soft night air. I wondered what the engineer could be blowing for.

The men were clambering aboard the flatcar behind us.

"All aboard, Matt," Chavez said, springing lightly down over the coal pile in the tender and landing beside me.

"Where have you been, Mex?" Kerlin growled, looking up. "You missed the work up here."

"Shut up, Mike!" I snapped.

"My name is Diego, señor," Chavez replied in a deadly ominous tone.

I shot a look at him in the dimness. It was the first time I had heard him respond to any of the jibes of the Irishman.

"Is that a fact, now?" Kerlin stood up.

"Dammit, shut up, both of you! You picked one helluva time to settle your differences. We have to get this train moving. Kerlin, grab that shovel and start stoking this firebox. Chavez, stand by to jump off and throw that switch when we get to the main line."

The two backed away from each other. Kerlin snatched the shovel out of the coal pile. Chavez slid over to the right side and put one foot down on the first step of the ladder.

I stripped off my jacket and hung it on a projecting knob, then wiped a sleeve across my eyes. Sweat was trickling down my sides under my shirt, not entirely due to the heat of the boiler in front of me.

What had Gil Latham told me? I struggled to remember his exact instructions. Carefully, I gripped the long reverse lever and eased it to forward motion. The rapid chuffing of the approaching locomotive grew louder as I reached for the parallel throttle lever in front of me. The train was coming fast, and I jerked the throttle open. The big driving wheels spun on the rails. We didn't move. I shoved the throttle closed, feeling like a fool. Then I *eased* it open, sweat dripping from my nose. The massive steel drivers took hold and we began to move.

Kerlin swung open the firebox door and hurled in a shovelful of coal. The red mouth gaped open, then slammed shut, cutting off the light as Kerlin dug in his shovel again. I leaned on the padded armrest and stuck my head out the side window, even though I had a tall, narrow window directly in front of me that gave a view along the catwalk to the front of the engine. I mainly needed the cool wind of our motion to fan my sweating face. We picked up speed — ten, fifteen, twenty. I dared not go too fast because the switch was coming up and I couldn't see. I squinted ahead. Why couldn't I see any better? Then I realized that I had forgotten to light the big coal-oil headlamp. We were running blind. Damn! How stupid! But there was no time for that now. We were risking a bad wreck by trying to beat that train to the switch. I was sure the other train was being run by a competent engineer. But they were running in reverse, and we had no lights.

Even if we did beat them out onto the main track but couldn't get the switch thrown back fast enough, they would crash. Of course, we could just throw the switch and let them run over it and derail, without ever risking ourselves. That would stop them. But there were two things wrong with that idea, I realized, as the thoughts raced through my mind. First, even though some of their men might be hurt or killed in the wreck, the rest of those hired guns would be after us with blood in their eyes. And secondly, we weren't out to destroy D&RG rolling stock or to kill anyone unnecessarily. Quite the opposite. We had been sent to capture and protect railroad property. One train was already wrecked, through no fault of ours.

I glanced to my left to get a look at the oncoming train. The eastern sky was beginning to lighten, and I could just make out the strange sight of the red-eyed caboose leading the train and the headlamp beam trailing behind like some thick, white tail.

"Slow down, Matt! Slow!" Diego's warning interrupted my thoughts. I had unconsciously opened the throttle lever and we were rolling even faster.

"The switch!"

I slammed the throttle lever forward. In my haste and inexperience, I locked the air brakes. An ungodly screech of steel wheels against steel rails assaulted our ears. Sparks flew. We were thrown forward as the engine suddenly slowed. Diego disappeared from the ladder beside me. We finally stopped a scant few yards from the switch. Chavez was already there, heaving the long lever up, over, and down. He stamped the switch handle firmly into place.

"Go!" he shouted.

I released the brakes and tried to control my adrenaline as I eased the throttle lever back, releasing steam into the cylinders. *Whoof! Whoof! Whoof!* The straight stack blasted smoke as our locomotive gathered her feet under her. The six big driving wheels took hold. Diego swung up onto the ladder beside me again, out of the spouting steam, as we rolled slowly past.

"Come on! Come on!" I gritted under my breath, trying to urge more speed into the tons of iron under us. We slowly gained momentum.

The tender blocked my view of the approaching train, but the urgent wailing of its steam whistle was ever louder as it bore down upon us. I could hear some shouting from the men on the flatcar behind.

The engine and tender were past the switch.

I looked back from my window seat. The flatcar was about to clear the switch when I heard a series of bangs. My heart jumped in my chest. We had been hit!

The frantic sound of the couplings banging continued as the engineer at the far end frantically applied his brakes. When I could see behind us, I knew we were not hit.

We were still accelerating, leaving the open switch behind us. There was no time for anyone to jump off and close it. If the other train could not stop, they would be derailed. I leaned far out the side window, trying to see. I could make out three dark figures on the rear platform of the red-lighted caboose. Someone was waving a lantern off this side of the platform. Two of the men jumped off to one side, and the third ran back inside the car as the train slowed. Then the end of the caboose tipped as it ran over the open switch and bumped slowly to a stop.

"Whew!" I drew my head in and exhaled a long sigh. I hadn't been aware of holding my breath. "They got 'er stopped, but the wheels of one truck are off the tracks."

"With a slow, steady pull, they should be able

to drag it back on the rails," DeArmand said, now alert and sitting on the stoker's seat opposite. Kerlin was climbing back up over the tender to have a better look. A minute later he was back.

"How's she look?"

"Not bad at all. They're signaling the engineer to pull back. Another man is standing by the switch."

"That won't slow them up much if —" I was interrupted by the unmistakable sound of three shots exploding somewhere behind. Then two more.

"Better keep your head in," I cautioned Kerlin. "I don't think those were our men shooting."

DeArmand quietly instructed Anderson, who was still in the cab, to shovel some coal into the firebox. I glanced at the steam gauge. It had dropped very slightly. I looked ahead. In the graying light, spreading up from the eastern horizon, the tracks ran straight and clear for at least two miles before dipping below my line of sight in a prairie swell.

I could imagine the confusion on the train behind us. Did they know who we were or what we were about? Had they stopped long enough at the wreck site to find out what had happened? Did they have any of our men prisoner aboard their coaches? I had to assume they knew all about us. They could have surprised and forced the information out of anybody they found at the wreck site. Maybe our men had driven them off; they were well armed.

"Diego, would you check to make sure nobody was hit by that gunfire?" I said.

He nodded silently and scrambled up the tender and over the back of the coal pile.

I opened the throttle wider, trying to coax more speed out of the big iron horse.

"If we can get a lead on them, we'll have time to stop and yank a rail up, or do something to stop them," I remarked aloud to Kerlin, DeArmand, and Anderson.

"No hope of making a standing fight of it," DeArmand said, his big shoulders a slumping silhouette in the opposite window with the reddening eastern sky behind him. "Hit and run is about all we can do."

"It will be enough," I answered, my confidence returning. "If we can delay them long enough, any fighting taking place at Pueblo will be over, and they won't be part of it. Those sixty gunmen have to be a good chunk of their fighting force."

Anderson slammed the firebox door shut and leaned on his shovel, wiping sweat from his broad face. "That may be, but they can still come down on us pretty hard. We have to stop sometime. I say our only hope for our own safety is to wreck that train."

I shook my head. "Not unless we absolutely have to. There will be sheriffs and deputized posses at Colorado Springs and Pueblo to give us a hand, as well as some of our own D and RG men."

Kerlin snorted. "I learned at Rorke's Drift to take whatever action I could to save myself and my fellows rather than wait and hope for some future rescue. I wouldn't be talking to you now if our few had waited for another regiment to head off those approaching Zulus. I say we do whatever we can to wreck that train behind us, and damn the consequences. We should do what we can to save ourselves."

"They may have some of our own men as captives on that train," I countered. "What good is a victory if we hand back General Palmer a pile of wrecked equipment?"

"We save ourselves," Kerlin growled.

Just then Chavez's dark figure climbed down into the cab. "One man hit in the arm. But they have stopped the blood. They are using the ties to build themselves a barricade."

"Ah, my little dark-skinned friend, you can beat the very devil out of your own hide during Lent, but you won't be for puttin' a few holes in them that would kill you *and* your friends. It's truly amazin' how you've survived in this land so long. Is it religious conviction, or are you just a wee bit afraid of someone with a gun?"

"Of course not, señor."

Did I detect a slight sneer in the calm voice?

"Right now, we need to get ourselves some breathing room," I said to break the tension between the two. "Then we'll decide what to do."

I eased back on the throttle some more, and the clumps of mesquite and creosote bush began to flash past on either side as the locomotive rocked back and forth on the narrow rails. I could hear the slight rhythmic pounding of the side rods as I drove her ahead.

DeArmand lifted his head from where he had pillowed it on his arms. "Give 'er a few more scoops," he said in a weak voice. Kerlin grabbed the scoop shovel and went to it.

"Scatter the next one around a little more," DeArmand said as Kerlin drove his scoop into the pile again.

"Right you are." The iron door opened and the burly Irishman bumped the edge of the fiery opening, spilling most of the coal on the footplate.

"Damn!" He drove his scoop into the pile again as the door clanged shut. This time he was successful and fanned the coal out evenly in the roaring interior.

"Good, good," DeArmand muttered weakly, dropping his head on his arms.

Kerlin kept stoking for a few minutes and then straightened up.

"Here you are, my man. Use your back for something besides the whip!" Kerlin snapped, tossing the shovel to Chavez, who was standing behind me. Diego was caught unprepared and the shovel skidded out the side of the cab and was gone.

"What the hell's wrong with you?" I shouted at Kerlin. "That was the only scoop shovel we had. Unless you want to stoke with your hands, you better get back on the flatcar and get one o' those long-handled digging shovels we brought along."

Apparently realizing that he had acted like a spoiled child, Kerlin obeyed without a word.

We surged along under full power for another two miles or more. Then the tracks started down a long, gentle grade.

"Wooden trestle coming up," I said, peering intently through the dirty glass of the narrow window in front of me.

"Good. We can stop on the other side and blow the bridge," Kerlin said. "That'll put a crimp in them."

"Did you bring any blasting powder?" I inquired. He shook his head disgustedly.

"Well, we don't have the time or the tools to dismantle it by hand."

"We must do something soon, señor," Diego offered. "We are not more than ten miles from Colorado Springs."

The light from the eastern horizon was spreading up over the vault of sky above us, chasing the darkness beyond the barrier of the Rockies, a few miles to the west. The light was good to see by, even though the sun had not yet shown the top of its head above the edge of the world.

"Diego, see how far back they are. We might

try to stop up ahead and yank up a rail."

The lithe Mexican was halfway up the tender before I had finished speaking.

I knew it was safer to slow down when crossing bridges and trestles, but I kept the throttle back and let it roll. We picked up speed on the downgrade and roared across the wooden structure that was hardly longer than our short train. By the time we began to slow somewhat on the opposite grade, Chavez was back.

"They are maybe three miles back, Matt. The men are ready when you are.

I nodded and kept the throttle wide open to gain the top of the grade before I stopped. The trestle was at the bottom of a long dip in the level land. If we could get up the other side to the flat land again, we would be out of the line of sight and fire from our pursuers for a short time.

But just as the grade leveled out, the tracks swept to the right in a long curve to avoid a copse of trees in a small gully. I was looking back and didn't see the curve until we were already into it. I thrust the throttle forward but could feel the engine leaning left into the curve as the right drive wheels lifted. Two things saved us from going off the narrow-gauge tracks. First, the long upgrade had cut our speed slightly. And second, the curve was not a sharp one. I held my breath for a few seconds until we settled back on our wheels and slowed.

I slowed further and finally applied the air brakes, and we ground to a halt.

The men were piling off the flatcar when I jumped down from the cab.

"Get one of those rails pried up!" I yelled, running back to join them. Willing hands took to the task with crowbars. But the job proved to be tougher than we expected. The spikes were driven deep into the green ties, some of which were wet. But our men were experienced hands. They put some leverage and muscle to it, and first one, and then another spike was drawn out.

I threw a glance at the pursuing train. It was just disappearing backward from my line of sight into the deep swale. Black smoke billowed above it as it plunged down the grade toward the trestle. We didn't have much time. But the work of getting the rail up started to go a little quicker.

We made one bad mistake. We all started from one end of the rail. And we encountered some stubborn spikes. The crowbars were short, which allowed only one man at a time to get leverage on them. The work was going agonizingly slowly.

"We'll never get this thing up in time," Sam Anderson said, coming up to me.

"Let's get hold of this loose end and see if we can bend it up. Maybe it will snap."

Anderson directed five of the men to get crowbars and shovels under the end we had freed. They levered it up enough to get their hands under it. But, even adding three more men, including me and Chavez, the combined strength of eight men could not bend the rail up enough to make any difference.

A sudden blast of a steam whistle raised the hair on the back of my neck. Jets of black smoke were staining the early morning sky. Suddenly, as I looked, the rear platform of the red caboose came rolling up out of the dip. Men with guns crammed the rear platform inside the iron railing.

"Jam something under that rail and get back aboard! Quick!"

Someone shoved the wooden handle of a shovel under the loosened end of the rail, and they all made a dash for the flatcar. I ran for the engine, along with Kerlin and Chavez. Anderson went with the men to the rear.

When I got back inside again, DeArmand was hobbling back and forth on his bad leg, trying to stoke the firebox to keep up the steam pressure. He was still dizzy and weak, but he had managed to get a few scoops of coal in.

"Thanks, DeArmand." I slid into my seat as Kerlin took the long-handled shovel from the fireman.

I released the air brakes and eased open the throttle. We began to move. Slowly. It took awhile to get up speed from a dead stop. And the train behind was rolling fast.

"DeArmand, do you feel strong enough to

take over this thing for a little while?" I asked.

He nodded weakly, but then I saw some of the old flash in his dark eyes. "You bet.

"Always wanted a chance to run one o' these things," he muttered as he slid into my right-hand seat and placed his hand on the throttle lever. I made sure he was alert before I climbed up the tender and over the coal pile, followed closely by Kerlin and Chavez.

Just as I topped the coal pile, a bullet rang off the iron back of the tender. I slammed on the brakes so fast, the loose coal rolled from under my feet and my legs shot out into space. I grabbed wildly for a handhold as I fell. One arm raked down the side of the car and my hand banged against the iron rung of the ladder. My fingers closed on it. The weight of my body nearly jerked my shoulder out of socket. I hung on desperately, twisting, until I could get my feet on the ladder. Then I was able to climb down and hop safely over to the flatcar. I sprawled on my stomach behind the barricade formed by the stacked ties and rubbed my wrenched shoulder. Our men were returning fire.

The pursuing train had topped the long grade and was rolling fast into the curve that had almost derailed me. On they came toward the rail we had loosened. I could see some wild activity and arm waving from the figures on the back platform as they saw the rail with one end bent up slightly. Any second I expected to see the caboose leave the tracks. But the rail was on the inside of the curve. And the speed of the train was throwing it to the outside, lifting the inside wheels slightly. The car rolled over the loosened rail and merely flattened it down into place again, apparently crushing the shovel handle we had wedged under it. But someone inside the caboose had evidently signaled the engineer — too late — to stop. The train slowed quickly and we began to pull away. By the time the train behind us had come to a complete stop, the locomotive had already passed over the bent rail, and the engineer almost immediately gave it a shot of steam. But, by then, we had opened a good quarter-mile gap on them. We had slowed them, but not for long.

I had my Colt in hand, but we had pulled well out of any effective pistol range. Two of our men still fired their carbines, but with the car rocking from side to side it would take a lucky shot to hit anything behind us.

In a silent explosion of fire and light, the sun had appeared over the eastern horizon. Another beautiful June day was beginning. But, except for the welcome light, we hardly noticed. I was more aware of the constant shower of fine ash and grit blowing back from our locomotive stack.

I got to my knees and, rubbing my wrenched shoulder, peered over the stack of ties. The caboose was coming on again and seemed to be getting closer, little by little, as I watched. The track had straightened out once more. As I stared at the end of the caboose, I suddenly realized that, in spite of their superior firepower, our pursuers were at a distinct disadvantage. As long as the tracks were reasonably straight, the gunmen could not get an angle of fire on us. The only ones who could get a bead on us had to stand on the rear platform of the caboose. And they had to expose themselves to our fire to do so. Only one man at a time could fit into the window of the cupola on top to get a clear line of fire. Any others who wanted to shoot had to lean out the side windows of the coaches.

As the space between us began to close again, our men began firing. One man with a Winchester squeezed off a shot next to me and let out a shout as a figure on the platform in the distance grabbed his thigh and fell.

With the noise of the wind and the engine and the firing, it was impossible to talk without shouting.

Either our pursuers had put on a tremendous burst of speed or we were slowing down, because they were definitely catching up — fast.

I swore quickly to myself. We had left no one to fire the engine for DeArmand! I shoved my Colt into its holster and staggered across the rocking platform toward the tender.

"No stoker!" I yelled at the curious glance Kerlin threw me.

"I'll go!" he shouted, waving me back.

He was up and over the tender in a flash. But we continued to slow down for several more minutes before steam pressure could be built back up. The pursuing train was closing the gap. I estimated we were running no more than twenty miles an hour. The men crouching behind the barricade of ties were getting nervous. Rifles began to crack from the platform of the caboose. Lead slugs flattened against the back of the tender and dug into the thick ties in front of us. We dared not show our heads.

There were only three rifles among the eleven of us. The rest were armed with pistols, but no one appeared to have much ammunition other than what he carried in the cartridge loops of his gun belt or a handful of extra shells in jacket pockets.

Colorado Springs surely couldn't be much farther. But what was happening there? If the town and depot had been taken or held by the Santa Fe forces, we might have to make a run straight through for our own safety. But we would have to stop soon and water up. I tried to remember where the next water tank was below Colorado Springs. I couldn't place it. Our run toward Denver last night had started out as an offensive operation, but had now turned into a defensive one.

"We've got to slow them up, somehow!" I said.

Sam Anderson, who was crouching nearby, glanced at me.

"Any suggestions?"

"Kick a few of these ties off in front of them."

"Hell, that's the only thing saving us from being shot."

"We might try throwing off a few of the tools," I suggested.

He pondered the idea. Several of the men were looking at us. They were used to being told what to do.

"Try heaving over that coil of wire."

Anderson seized the coil in a big fist, sighted through a gap in the ties, and arched it over his head. The coil hit on edge, bounced, and rolled off the track before the caboose came close to it.

"Nothing left but some shovels and small crowbars," Anderson said.

I eyed the odds and ends of tools that lay scattered about among us. Even two sledgehammers would be of no use. There seemed to be nothing that would slow down that onrushing train.

"The ties."

"What?"

"The ties," I repeated. "We can kick a few ties off the back. They'll have to stop and clear the tracks. That will slow them down."

"These ties are all the protection we've got," Anderson objected.

"A couple of us can keep 'em busy while the men get back into the tender. And there's room for a couple o' men in the cab. C'mon, we've got to hurry!" I said, glancing through a crack at the caboose that was a bare fifty yards behind us.

"Okay," Anderson agreed reluctantly. He quickly passed the word among the others.

"Ready?" I raised my Colt, and Anderson gripped his carbine.

"Now!"

We both rose up as one and began blazing away. The wind whipped the sounds and smoke of the blasts away as our men scrambled toward the tender. There was a sudden panic among the crowded figures on the caboose platform as the slugs smashed into the wooden car and whanged off the ironwork. By the time they got back inside the car, or crouched down and began returning our fire, most of our men had scampered up and over the back of the tender and were out of sight. Anderson and I fired until our weapons were empty.

"That took 'em by surprise," I remarked as I punched the empty shells out of my Colt. He nodded. Bullets thudded into the ties and ripped up splinters from the wooden floor of the open car.

"What now?" Anderson asked. "It's just you and me and these ties."

I holstered my Colt. "Here goes."

I selected a tie at the edge of our little breastworks, sat back, and kicked with both feet. The tie skidded off the end of the car and hit the track, bouncing end over end and then off to one side.

I dragged off another one, as Anderson pumped a couple of shots to keep them occupied. I pushed the tie off the back with my feet as square as I could. But the wood hit, bounced, and skipped off to one side. The same thing happened with the next four ties. It seemed impossible to get the ties to land across the rails. Finally, a tie bounced, skidded, and came to rest on the outside of the tracks with one end tilted up over a rail.

The train had begun to slow when the engineer first saw what we were attempting to do. As they approached the tie, one of the men reached down with a rifle and knocked the end of the tie aside as they came up to it. We had gained distance on them, and Anderson and I took advantage of this to make a break for the tender ourselves, since our supply of ties was nearly gone, and with them our protection.

Anderson tossed his empty rifle up onto the coal pile and went up after it. I was right on his heels.

"Any luck?" DeArmand asked, looking up from the engineer's seat where he still held the throttle. Our speed was gradually picking up as Kerlin hurled shovelful after shovelful of coal into the fiery maw of the firebox door.

"Not much. We slowed 'em up some. But they're coming on again."

"Any coal oil left?" DeArmand asked.

"About a gallon."

"Splash it over that flatcar, set 'er afire, and then unhitch the car. That should keep 'em off for a while."

"Good idea." I grabbed the can.

"I'll do it," Kerlin said quickly. "I may be shovelin' coal in the hereafter, but I've had me fill of it for now." He handed his shovel to the man who stood nearest and wiped his sleeve across his red, sweating face.

Before anyone could object, he grabbed the can of coal oil. A few seconds later those of us lying on our stomachs on the coal watched as he jumped down onto the swaying platform of the flatcar, yanked the cork out of the jug spout, and began sloshing the fuel back and forth as he backed up. When it was empty, he tossed the can over our heads where it clanked into the foot-plate of the cab, nearly hitting a man. Crouching at the forward end of the car, he fished in his pocket and attempted to strike a match. Then another. Both blew out before he could touch either to the fuel-wet wood. He tried yet a third match — with the same result.

"He needs a torch!" someone yelled down into the cab. Several men glanced about, but nothing presented itself. Finally, the man who was shoveling coal with the long-handled shovel retrieved the coal-oil can, dripped a few remaining drops on the end of the wooden handle. Then he opened the firebox door and shoved the handle into the flames. It was ablaze instantly. He yanked it out, and thrusting the burning handle behind a projecting pipe on the boiler, snapped the end of the handle off with one quick jerk. Then he passed the burning torch up to us and it was handed on down to Kerlin. He tossed it. The flatcar caught slowly, then blazed up in the breeze until the red caboose a hundred yards back almost disappeared in a shimmering wall of flame.

The wind was whipping the flames away from him as Kerlin stepped carefully down to the bottom of the iron ladder on the back of the tender. Placing one foot on the bottom rung, he stretched out and put the other on the rocking edge of the flatcar. Hanging on with one hand, he reached down with the other and began tugging at the pin. But nothing happened. After several seconds, he straightened up to rest. Then he went at it again.

"Hit the brakes, DeArmand!" somebody yelled.

The engineer glanced back curiously. I nodded emphatically. He eased off the throttle and pulled back on the air brake lever. The strain was eased on the coupling as the trailing car came forward. Chavez and I were lying side by side on the top edge of the coal pile, looking over and down at Kerlin.

The pin came partway out as he jerked on it. Before he could pull again, a blast of gunfire came from the gaining train. Kerlin's big frame jerked sideways and fell, clawing for a hold as he dropped between the cars. He was conscious and clutched the coupling as he fell underneath, his legs dragging on the ties between the wheels of the flatcar.

Chavez leapt over the back of the tender and down onto the end of the flatcar as nimble as a cat. He lay down just at the edge, perilously close to the flames that were blowing back. He hooked one leg around the upright rod that held the brake wheel. Then he leaned down with both arms and tried to grip Kerlin's arms, which were wrapped around the coupling from underneath.

"Stop! Stop! Stop the engine!" voices around me were yelling.

"Not too fast! You'll jerk his hands loose!"

Chavez was straining with all his might to reach the dragging man. Looking straight down, I could see the bloodless fingers slipping loose as his boots and legs dragged and bounced on the rough cross ties. I didn't know how badly wounded the big man was, but I held my breath as one of Kerlin's hands slipped off. Just as the other hand was jarred loose, Chavez made a wild stab, caught the sleeve of Kerlin's jacket, and hung on desperately with one hand. The Irishman was taking a terrific pounding, and the bouncing was tearing his sleeve loose.

Chavez eased his leg loose from the brake wheel rod and slid himself down to straddle the jerking coupling, all the while holding a handful of jacket in one viselike fist. Then he bent down and gripped Kerlin's arms with both hands.

The train was coming to a halt gradually, and we were only moving about ten miles an hour.

I saw Diego's shirt back bulge as his muscles coiled into knots with the effort. But there was no way the smaller Mexican from his precarious perch could drag the heavy Kerlin out from under. The best he could do was hold him from slipping under the wheels.

The locomotive finally ground to a halt in a hiss of steam. I was the first down the ladder, followed by two other men. We crowded each other to pull Kerlin out to one side between the cars.

Without the wind to fan the flames away, the heat was searing, and the fire was spreading to engulf the entire wooden flatcar.

"Here they come!"

Two pistols exploded over my head at the train that was closing fast.

Kerlin was battered and bloody, his canvas trousers in shreds. One thigh was soaked in blood, apparently where he had taken a bullet. His eyes were slitted. He looked to be semi-conscious.

I yanked my Colt and fired twice at the approaching caboose.

Chavez grabbed Kerlin under the arms and somehow wrestled him up and over his shoulder. Then, staggering under the weight on the uneven ground, he went forward to the steps of the engine cab where several willing hands hauled the Irishman up onto the foot-plate.

Anderson, meanwhile, had pulled the coupling pin.

"Go!"

"Move it!" we were yelling.

DeArmand gave her a shot of steam. The wheels spun and took hold. Anderson and I raced alongside and leapt for a handhold on the iron ladder of the engine.

Gunfire was coming from the Santa Fe men behind us, but they had to slow to take up the burning flatcar.

Several of us were crowded into the cab, where Kerlin was stretched out on his back. Before we had even gotten up speed again, DeArmand yelled, "There's Colorado Springs!"

We were ten more minutes getting there. From two miles or so away we could see knots of riders milling around the steep-roofed depot. DeArmand hauled down on the overhead whistle cord with a series of short, urgent bursts and several long wails. He kept this up until we were flashing past the depot, smothering the platform in clouds of smoke and steam. He eased off the throttle and gradually applied the air brakes, but by the time we ground to a halt, we were a hundred yards past the station.

All of us except DeArmand swarmed off both

sides of the engine and sprinted back up the tracks. Rifle barrels bristled from every shuttered window of the depot. About a dozen deputies and a company of uniformed riders had the building surrounded. A detachment of horsemen broke off and trotted toward the passenger train that was slowing to a stop with the burning flatcar. As I got closer, I recognized the insignia of Company B of the First Colorado Cavalry. They were well armed and looked grimfaced as they covered the windows and platforms of the slowing train.

The cavalry had the men on the following train disarmed within minutes. They filed off the coaches, hands raised.

The Santa Fe men barricaded inside the depot, after seeing their unexpected reinforcements captured, decided it was hopeless and gave up without a struggle.

We carried Kerlin to the hotel and rounded up the town's only doctor. By noon we were all sitting down to a dinner in the hotel dining room — a victory dinner General Palmer called it, although the issue was far from settled in Pueblo.

But by three-thirty that afternoon, it was all over. Chavez and I, Anderson, General Palmer, and several of the men from our train were crowded into Kerlin's hotel room, where he was propped up in bed spooning up some broth we had brought him. He was bruised from head to foot, bleeding from dozens of cuts, and had a possible fractured heel. The doctor had treated him and gone. His heavily bandaged right leg lay atop the covers. The rifle slug had passed through the thigh muscle without hitting a bone or an artery. He had been lucky.

"Good news!" General Palmer's harried telegrapher rushed into the room waving a message. "Just came over the wire. The sheriff and a posse of about two hundred local citizens have taken the roundhouse at Pueblo. Rousted out Bat Masterson and his gunmen from Dodge. They had to bust a few heads to do it, and one man was shot in the butt climbing out the window, but all of the D and RG property is back in our hands!"

A cheer went up from the small assembly.

Kerlin grinned and set his empty bowl on the table beside him. He shifted his position on the pillows with obvious pain. But then he reached over and offered his hand to Diego Chavez, who stood nearby. He looked somewhat startled but finally put out his hand and gripped Kerlin's.

"*Gracias,* my friend," Kerlin murmured in his Irish brogue. *"Amigos?"*

Diego's dark face was impassive for a few moments and he withdrew his hand. He turned away. But he turned back and nodded to the injured man just before he went out the door.

We hope you have enjoyed this Large Print book. Other G.K. Hall & Co. or Chivers Press Large Print books are available at your library or directly from the publishers.

For more information about current and upcoming titles, please call or write, without obligation, to:

Publisher
G.K. Hall & Co.
295 Kennedy Memorial Drive
Waterville, ME 04901
Tel. (800) 223-1244
Tel. (800) 223-6121

OR

Chivers Press Limited
Windsor Bridge Road
Bath BA2 3AX
England
Tel. (0225) 335336

All our Large Print titles are designed for easy reading, and all our books are made to last.